S...
CHA...
THE SAFE HOUSE
IN MALIBU HILLS WAS
ANYTHING BUT . . .

He slowly opened the door, cautiously peered out into the dawn. Kee Nang stepped outside, stopped in front of him, standing very close. Grasping Chandler's hand tightly, she led him due east into the rising sun.

They passed two dead guards. One of the men had a knife buried to the hilt in his chest; the other had a deep gash completely encircling his twisted, broken neck.

The monkey man's whip had killed the second man, Chandler thought, and shuddered.

Suddenly Kee Nang stopped. Chandler reached out to grip her arm, then felt his breath catch in his throat.

Ten feet in front of them, a black mist oozed up from the ground, eclipsing the bars of sunlight shining through the trees behind it. There was a sharp, hissing sound, and an instant later Sardo Numspa—impeccably dressed in his gray suit, cape, and black English riding boots with gold spurs—stepped out of the cloud of fetid gas.

"Good morning, sports fans," Sardo Numspa said, and grinned triumphantly.

THE GOLDEN CHILD™

a novel by
GEORGE C. CHESBRO

based upon an
original screenplay by
DENNIS FELDMAN

PUBLISHED BY POCKET BOOKS NEW YORK

Another *Original* publication of POCKET BOOKS

POCKET BOOKS, a division of Simon & Schuster, Inc.
1230 Avenue of the Americas, New York, N.Y. 10020

ISBN: 0-671-63039-3

First Pocket Books printing December, 1986

10 9 8 7 6 5 4 3 2 1

POCKET and colophon are registered trademarks of Simon & Schuster, Inc.

TM designates a Trademark of Paramount Pictures Corporation.

® designates a Trademark of Paramount Pictures Corporation Registered in the U.S. Patent and Trademark Office.

Printed in the U.S.A.

But down these mean streets a man must go who is not himself mean, who is neither tarnished nor afraid. The detective in this kind of story must be such a man. He is the hero; he is everything. He must be a complete man and a common man and yet an unusual man. He must be, to use a rather weathered phrase, a man of honor—by instinct, by inevitability, without thought of it, and certainly without saying it. He must be the best man in his world and a good enough man for any world.

—RAYMOND CHANDLER

Chapter One

THE SMALL BROWN BIRD, APPEARING LIKE A MOTE OF DUST on a vast tapestry of cloudless blue sky, fluttered its wings. It struggled to ascend in the thin, cold Tibetan air to flee the menacing figures below. In the distance, crowning a soaring peak, a golden temple gleamed in the sunlight. A great horn boomed like a sigh of God, its sound rolling and echoing through the surrounding labyrinth of mountain passes like thunder.

Then the golden temple winked from the bird's sight as strong air currents slammed into her frail back, inexorably forcing her down toward the procession of men and mountain ponies working their tortuous way up a narrow, jagged trail cut into the steep mountain-side.

Leading the ominous procession was a fair-skinned, reddish-haired man who was at least a head taller than the others. Dressed like a modern Italian count in the most stylish European clothing, his elegant appearance was accentuated by the cloth overcoat he wore draped over his shoulder. The pellucid air about him seemed to darken and shimmer with his passage, as if he were the bow of a ship of evil which tainted everything it touched.

Behind Sardo Numspa rode Fu, a figure who appeared more monkey than man, with a flat face and thick, glossy black hair which grew low on his forehead in a pronounced widow's peak. Coiled around Fu's chest was one of the most vicious weapons of the Chinese martial arts, a nine-sectioned steel whip.

A barrel-chested man wearing a robe ornamented with skulls carried a spear, which he occasionally used to prod his skittish mount; a young, thuggish-looking Oriental dressed in a rock band T-shirt and a leather flight jacket carried curved swords in zebra-skin sheaths crossed on his back; four squat Orientals, bearers dressed in dirty sheepskin *chubas,* carried a steel cage suspended between them by wooden poles.

The air around the steel cage, like that around Sardo Numspa, shimmered a dirty brown, as if the cage, with its lattice-work of coiling, sinister symbols, was the heart of the evil ship.

Bringing up the rear of the malevolent procession was Yu, a eunuch dressed in the clothes of a nineteenth-century Mandarin courtier and carrying a Chinese short crossbow made of aluminum and fiberglass. Beside Yu rode Til, a mountain of a man with a large, leathery callus on his forehead.

The bird renewed her struggles to fly away, but could not. A gust of icy wind buffeted the undersides of her wings, tossing her in the air. Losing control, she plummeted from the sky, desperately tried to veer, swooped through a circular opening in the side of the ominous cage. Suddenly the small brown bird was colder than she had ever been, and she knew she would die unless she could escape from the cage. Feebly fluttering her tiny wings, screaming from the cold which seemed to skewer her, she flew toward an opening on the far side of the cage—but the opening receded at her approach.

She veered to her right, but managed only to smash into the steel bars; there appeared to be more than ample space between the bars for her tiny body to slip through, but gelid winds of terrible force blew into her face, hurling her back each time she approached the side of the cage. She wheeled around, flew in panic in the opposite direction—and again smashed into cold, hard steel. Terrified, she beat her wings against the metal until she felt her bones snap like dry twigs in the paralyzing cold.

Then everything in her cracked, shattered, and she left the evil cage, a shapeless wad of blood and feathers falling through a hole in the bottom, escaping only in death . . .

The great horn boomed again, but this time there was a tiny silver bell tinkling in its sonic heart. A minuscule flame of hope flickering in the eternal, velvet night of eternity.

It was time for the tests, a quest for miracles, to begin.

Both sides of the Great Hall inside the golden temple were lined with purple-robed monks whose heads were shaved. Their soft chanting filled the hall, and seemed to vibrate with expectancy. The faces of all the monks

11

were turned toward an apse at the far end of the Great Hall where a naked boy-child of four or five unconcernedly played on a thick, purple mat plaited and woven from the finest materials.

Again the great horn boomed, the tiny bell chimed.

And the chanting abruptly stopped. Attendants appeared to dress the child in golden robes which caught and magnified the soft, yellow light of the butter lamps shining in the semi-darkness, suffusing the child, who now sat quietly in the lotus posture on a golden cushion in a quiet, radiant glow. The attendants stepped back into darkness, and four presiding officials emerged to stand behind the child.

A monk, carrying a silver tray which held four shiny toy balls made of multicolored thread, appeared at the opposite end of the hall and walked slowly down between the lines of monks. When he reached the figures at the end, he bowed, presenting the tray to the boy. Without hesitation the child at the center of the golden glow reached out and touched one of the balls.

There was a visible relaxation of tension among the four officials standing behind the child, and the eldest gave a brief nod to the monk with the tray to confirm that the boy-child had passed the first test. The monk set the ancient ball of thread down next to the child, then stepped away into the surrounding darkness.

Outside the temple, its echo pealing across the surrounding mountaintops, the great horn boomed; inside the temple, the tiny silver bell chimed.

A second monk appeared, carrying a tray containing four sets of rosary beads. The child ignored the tray when it was offered to him, and instead reached up and removed the rosary beads from around the monk's neck, to drape them around his own.

Even before the eldest monk gave his nod of confirmation, a murmur of knowing and astonishment rose from the monks gathered in the hall.

Yet again the boom of the horn, the tinkle of the tiny bell.

A third monk appeared. This man carried a wooden tray on which was arrayed four dead birds, all brilliantly colored, but with their tropical plumage now ragged and folded against their bodies, their legs stiffly outstretched.

The child reached out and touched one of the still bodies. Instantly, the small creature burst free from the bonds of death and leaped into the still, glass-like air of the temple as the monks and the boy-child laughed and cheered, applauding its resurrection and its soaring, swooping passage over their heads. The bird flew as it had never flown before, sang as it had never sung, her deep-throated trills providing harmony and counterpoint to the cheers and laughter of the people below, her triumphant song a salute to the golden child.

Without warning, the great wood and steel doors at the far end of the hall burst open with a crash that pealed like thunder and pierced the hearts of the gathered monks. A blast of frigid air swept through the hall, billowing the purple robes of the monks, buffeting the resurrected bird.

Then Sardo Numspa and his raiders entered, and the carnage began.

The raiders slaughtered mercilessly, systematically. Steel crossbow arrows flew through the air, burying themselves in the hearts of the monks. The Oriental thug in the leather jacket and rock band T-shirt whipped the twin swords from their sheaths on his back and began to slash; the swords, with their serrated edges, left gaping, jagged-edged wounds which resembled the open mouths of sharks. The blades flashed; hands, arms, legs, heads flew through the air, spewing fountains of blood . . .

The fearsome giant with the massive callus on his forehead used it to smash faces and skulls; again and again he would pull a helpless monk to him with his powerful arms, then snap his callused forehead forward, splintering bone, squashing features . . .

Fu, the monkey man, slouched through the hall, his terrible, nine-sectioned steel whip snapping out again and again to break necks and bones, lay open flesh, sever limbs . . .

The man with the skulls on his robe speared one monk, then another. And another . . .

Sardo Numspa, his night-black, pupilless eyes smoldering like black flame, strolled calmly through the carnage, seemingly oblivious to the blood and screams all around him, his fine clothes untouched by the gore which filled the air of the Great Hall like crimson rain. He stopped before the golden child, who stared back up at the man, obviously fearful—but also defiant.

Suddenly an arrow came flying through the air, on a direct line with the boy-child's heart; at the last moment, the arrow veered sharply away from the golden child and buried itself in the wall behind the boy.

"Bring the cage," Numspa commanded, his thick, black eyebrows raised slightly as he studied the arrow which still quivered in the thick wood of the wall a few feet away.

The four Tibetan bearers shuffled quickly forward, set down the deadly cage near the boy.

"The child is protected," Sardo Numspa said as he made a slight motion with his right hand. Twelve sinister, metal arms snapped out from the sides of the cage to create an enlarged opening at the bottom. "He possesses great power; don't let him touch you."

Suddenly a monk, in a desperate effort to protect the child, rushed forward—only to be skewered by the spear of the robed raider. As the raider yanked his spear from the monk's chest he lost his balance and stumbled backward toward the child, who reached up and gently touched the man's hand.

Instantly, the raider was transformed: the hate in his face and eyes melted to love, contempt to compassion. Without hesitation he lunged forward and speared one of the bearers, who crashed backward into the cage, rocking it with a clang that echoed throughout the Great Hall.

The transformed raider speared a second bearer, then stepped back and stood defiantly, spear raised, in front of the golden child even as the other raiders—steel whip, crossbow, jagged-edged swords raised—began slowly to converge on him. Sensing that he must die, the transformed raider suddenly gripped his spear with both hands and lunged at Sardo Numspa.

But Sardo Numspa was no longer there; there was a wink of dirty brown light, and the point of the spear passed through air. Another wink of light, and the man with black fire eyes appeared against the wall, next to the embedded arrow.

An instant later an arrow pierced the transformed raider's heart, killing him instantly.

"No witnesses," Numspa said matter-of-factly as he stepped away from the wall and once again approached the boy-child, whose head and body were bowed in sorrow.

The steel whip snapped, swords flashed, arrows flew

as the last of the monks, along with the two remaining bearers, were ruthlessly murdered.

"No witnesses," Numspa repeated with a grunt of satisfaction, then motioned curtly with his left hand.

The monkey man and the giant lifted the deadly cage, then slowly lowered it over the boy. Instantly, the glow around the child diminished, flickering down to a dull gleam, like faint sunlight on tarnished brass. The twelve arms of the cage snapped shut with an ominous clang of finality. Then the cage was lifted and the raiding party, led by Sardo Numspa, proceeded back through a horrid landscape of bleeding, torn bodies toward the great, open doors which gaped like a wound in the sky.

Behind, all that was left alive in the Great Hall was a small bird with brilliant plumage which perched high in the rafters, shivering with cold and terror.

Chapter Two

CHANDLER JARRELL JAYWALKED ACROSS SANTA MONICA, stepped around a man in a chicken suit who was hopping around on the sidewalk to advertise a new fast food franchise, walked halfway up the block and stopped in front of a telephone pole. He slipped a hammer from a loop in his belt, took a nail from his shirt pocket and proceeded to tack up one more of the posters he carried under his arm. When he had finished, he wiped sweat from his face with the back of his hand, squinted against the glare of the sun and studied the face of the 16-year-old girl in the poster.

Cheryl Mosely was an attractive, young lady, he thought, stepping to one side to avoid a glassy-eyed woman in a red lace body suit who brushed against his shoulder as she headed for the sex shop behind him. The photograph had come from a high school year-

17

book, and showed a freckle-faced girl with a long neck, high cheekbones and large eyes smiling confidently at the world. She'd already been gone a week before the girl's parents had called him in, Chandler thought, closing his sore eyes and rubbing them with his knuckles. God knew where she was now, and Chandler had lost His phone number a long time ago.

God, indeed.

Still rubbing his eyes, absently studying the tiny chemical explosions erupting on the backs of his eyelids, Chandler suddenly sensed that he was not alone.

He took his hands away from his eyes and was startled to find a woman standing only inches away from him. She was as tall as he was, just under six feet; she was Oriental—Chinese, Japanese, or perhaps Korean. She was dressed in an electric blue silk blouse, faded jeans and sneakers; her raven black hair was cut in bangs across her forehead, but fell in gleaming tresses across her shoulders. Large, limpid eyes as black as her hair studied him from a face that was not so much beautiful as handsome, with a strong chin and sensual lips that were now set in a firm line. Although the woman was slender—almost willowy—there was something about the way she carried herself that suggested to Chandler movement even while she was standing still, grace, speed and power. He put her age at around twenty-five.

He'd been twenty-five once, Chandler thought. A lifetime ago. Five years.

"Mr. Jarrell?"

"Right," Chandler replied cautiously. "Who are you?"

"My name is Kee Nang. I'm sorry I startled you."

"You can startle me any time." Chandler paused,

grinned. "I really hope you're trying to pick me up. This could be your lucky day."

"I would like to hire you, Mr. Jarrell."

"To do what?"

"To do what you do—find a child."

Chandler's grin vanished. "Runaway?"

"No. The boy is only five years old. He was kidnapped."

"Oh, Jesus," Chandler said, feeling an all-too-familiar pain in his stomach as his muscles knotted. "I'm sorry, lady. Your child?"

"No. Ours."

"*Ours?*" Chandler took a step backward. "Look, if this is some kind of paternity scam, it's really not worth your—"

"I didn't bear him."

Chandler studied the woman's face, the large eyes, the sensuous mouth. There was fear in the woman, he thought, held in check by quiet strength and dignity. "Have the police uncovered any leads at all?"

"No, Mr. Jarrell."

"What do the police say?"

"The police weren't notified."

"I don't understand."

"The police wouldn't be of any help to us, Mr. Jarrell, even if they believed. You're the only one who can help us."

"Believed?" The pain in Chandler's stomach was being rapidly displaced by a sour mix of doubt and suspicion. "Why wouldn't they believe this kid was snatched? When did it happen?"

"Five days ago. In Northeastern Tibet."

"Northeastern Tibet? Is that some new enclave? I know Beverly Hills, the Hollywood Hills, the Valley—"

"Tibet, Tibet, Mr. Jarrell."

Chandler blinked. *"That* Tibet?"

"That Tibet," the woman said quietly. "We have good reason to believe that the child is being held somewhere in Los Angeles."

Shit, Chandler thought. A good-looking, sad loony was just what he needed to go with the headache he was developing. "Excuse me, lady," he said, turning toward the entrance to the sex shop. "I'd love to stand around and chat with you, but I'm busy. Why don't you contact the local Tibetan Fraternal Association with your problem? This is Los Angeles, so there's bound to be one around someplace. Just check the telephone directory."

"Please, Mr. Jarrell," the woman said in a voice that could barely be heard above the noise of the traffic on the street, but nonetheless caused Chandler to stop. "You choose to appear rude, but I know that you're not a rude man."

Chandler slowly turned back to face the woman who called herself Kee Nang. Over her shoulder, on the opposite side of the street, a hitchhiking punk with spiked, orange hair was climbing into the back seat of a Mercedes Benz; beyond that, behind a fence, a bikini-clad woman on skis was snowplowing down a moving, carpeted ramp. "Sorry, lady. I haven't been sleeping too well lately."

"I don't understand," the woman said in the same soft, sibilant voice that was almost a whisper. "Won't you listen to me, please? It will only take five minutes of your time, and surely you can spare that."

"I'd only be humoring you, lady, and neither of us needs that."

"Why do you find it so difficult to believe I come from Tibet? Is it because I speak what I'm told is fairly good English? I assure you, there are many people in Tibet who speak fine English."

"Do they sell a lot of Adidas sneakers in Tibet?"

"I really have no idea," the woman said, looking down at her feet. "I bought these here. Would you be more inclined to believe me if I'd come to you dressed in a robe, beads and sandals?"

Chandler thought about it, shook his head. "No—then I'd be certain you were a local girl, probably born in West Hollywood. You have a point. You say this child was kidnapped in Tibet?"

"Yes. The boy is special."

"Sure," Chandler said with a shrug. "There are a few people like myself who'll tell you that all children are special."

"Indeed. Like all children, this boy-child is special; unlike other children, he happens to be the spiritual leader of two hundred million people in China, Tibet, and Southeast Asia."

"Ahhh," Chandler said as he felt the sour sensation in his stomach return and intensify. "Now I think I'm beginning to understand what this is all about: you want me to make a contribution."

The girl dismissed Chandler's words with an impatient gesture. Unruffled, she held her head high and her shoulders back in a posture of almost defiant dignity. "Four hundred years ago, the Nechung Oracle of our land predicted that the *Gompen Tarma*—that is Tibetan for 'Golden Child'—would be taken to a city in a new world, a 'city of angels.' The Oracle also predicted that the child could be rescued by a man who"—the woman paused, and the thin smile that tugged at the corners of her full lips was bittersweet—"was not exactly an angel himself."

A blond teenager no more than thirteen or fourteen in high heels, hot pants and a motorcycle jacket cut between them on the sidewalk, and Chandler quickly snatched a poster from under his arm and held it out in front of her. The girl glanced at the picture of Cheryl Mosely, shook her head and walked on.

"Certain omens are unmistakable, Mr. Jarrell," the woman with the blue-black hair and limpid eyes continued in the same even tone. "In all the world, there is only a single Chosen One—you. We've had computers throw the I Ching for every person in the Los Angeles phone book. You were picked independently by all three computers—in New York, London, and Delhi. It is your profession to find missing children; it is your destiny to find the Golden Child."

"Yeah," Chandler said, and sighed wearily. His headache was now full-blown, pressing painfully against the backs of his eyes. "La—Kee Nang? Is that your name?"

"Yes."

"Tell me, Kee Nang, what's your destiny? I mean, what does this religious outfit you belong to call itself? What do you believe? What is it about you people that sets you apart from the ten thousand or so other religious outfits in the world?"

"My destiny is to do everything in my power to try and see that you fulfill yours—and I see that you don't believe a word I'm saying."

"Come on, Kee Nang. Why would someone kidnap a child in Tibet and bring him all the way to Los Angeles?"

"Because the people who took the *Gompen Tarma* are sure no one here will believe us."

"Then they made a big mistake. There are loads of people around here who'll believe you; I'm just not one of them."

"They are sure no one who *matters* will believe us. In Los Angeles, I'm told, there are so many people who believe anything and everything that some wise men and women come to believe nothing."

"Kee Nang," Chandler said quietly, "there are a lot of private investigators in this city, and not a few of them will be most happy to work on a *per diem* basis scouring Los Angeles for your Golden Child, for as long as your heart desires and your money holds out."

"But you're not one of them."

"No."

"You won't help us?"

"No, ma'am." Chandler paused, hefted the posters under his arm. "I already have a job. This kid exists."

He hoped.

"But you haven't even asked how much we're willing to pay. It could be a substantial amount."

"It doesn't make any difference. If somebody offered me money to run laps around the Coliseum for a week, I wouldn't do that either. I don't want to waste my time on your religious fantasy, and I don't want to be responsible for you wasting your money."

"Mr. Jarrell, finding the *Gompen Tarma* is, quite literally, more important than anything else in the world."

"Excuse me, ma'am," Chandler said, turning and heading into the sex shop. "I have to go now."

Chapter Three

CHANDLER LET THE DOOR OF THE DIMLY LIT SHOP BANG shut behind him. The air inside the shop smelled of nervous sweat, tension, the bitter scent of impossible, crippling fantasies.

"Hey, pal, you back again?"

Chandler turned, looked up to where an obese man with an acne-scarred face sat on a raised platform behind a huge glass display case packed with rubber, leather and plastic sexual paraphernalia. Despite the hum of air conditioning equipment, it was overly warm in the shop, and the sweat on the fat man's face shimmered with an eerie glow, like tainted mercury, in the garish red fluorescent lighting.

"I've got another poster," Chandler said. "Mind if I put it up?"

The fat man with the DayGlo sweat shrugged. "Suit yourself."

Chandler walked past racks of books, magazines and video cassettes to a door leading to the live peep show section. The week before he had tacked up three posters of three different girls on the door, and now they were gone. The door was bare.

"What happened to the ones I put up last time?!" Chandler called across the shop.

"How the hell should I know?" the man behind the counter replied around a thick cigar he had just put in his mouth. "I let you put up those posters because I consider it my civic duty to help find missing kids. But, like I told you, we don't do no underage stuff here—don't take 'em as customers, and don't use 'em for the peepers."

"That's bullshit," Chandler replied evenly. "What about Mary Beth Hart?"

"Who's Mary Beth Hart?"

"She's the fourteen-year-old you had working the booths back here."

"Oh, yeah—I remember you saying something like that to me. Did you find your girl back there?"

"Nope. Somebody tipped me that she was here; obviously, somebody tipped her that I was coming here after her."

"I don't use no underage girls here, pal. You want to put up your posters, go ahead. Keep your accusations to yourself."

Chandler tacked up a poster of Cheryl Mosely, then turned back toward the other man and noisily jangled the quarters he always carried in his pockets when he was cruising the sex shops. "Well, that's done," he said easily. "Now I think I'll catch a few of the shows."

"Hey, pal, I know you're not a peeper," the fat man said, removing the cigar from his mouth and glaring at Chandler. "I let you put your poster up, and I'm telling you you're not going to find anything that interests you back there. Why the hell don't you go about your own business?"

"It's time for my coffee break," Chandler replied, and pushed through the door into a murky corridor, which was lined on both sides by curtained booths where, by dropping a quarter in a slot, a patron was treated to thirty seconds' worth of a stripper, behind a thick pane of glass, in various stages of undress; after thirty seconds, the scene behind the glass went dark.

The first cubicle was occupied.

"Excuse me, sir," Chandler said, pressing a dollar bill into the startled patron's hand as he pushed him to one side and bent down to peer through the viewer; the woman in the room behind the glass was middle-aged, with a ridiculous red wig that was too small for her. "Sorry," Chandler mumbled, and went back out into the corridor.

He was checking out his third booth when he heard a phone ringing somewhere deeper in the bowels of the building. Chandler had a pretty good idea what the ringing phone meant, and he dashed out of the cubicle he was in, turned left and started running toward the glowing red Exit sign at the end of the corridor. Suddenly a burly young man in a studded leather jacket stepped from behind a curtain and stood in the middle of the corridor, blocking Chandler's path.

"Hey, my man," the figure in the leather jacket said as he raised his hands, "just slow down a second and—"

Without breaking stride Chandler barreled into the

man as he had once barreled into would-be tacklers as a halfback at U.S.C., knocking the man off his feet and back through the curtain. Chandler kicked open the exit door, squinted and winced as the bright sunlight hit him in the face like a hammer.

He heard the sound of running feet on the gravel parking lot at the rear of the building. He glanced to his left in time to see Mary Beth Hart, dressed in a hot pink tube top and skintight jeans and accompanied by a young man who looked to be nineteen or twenty, run into the mouth of an alley. Trying to ignore his splitting headache, Chandler sprinted after them.

"*Mary Beth! Mary Beth!* Wait a minute! I want to talk to you!"

Chandler cursed to himself as the young man slowed his stride just long enough to half turn and raise his middle finger before disappearing up the alley along with the girl. Chandler, arms pumping at his sides, picked up his pace. He sprinted to the end of the alley, where he found the girl and young man tortuously working their way across the street as cars, horns blaring, screeched to a halt just inches from them. Taking advantage of the fact that traffic was already snarled, Chandler darted into the street, weaving his way through the cars to a renewed, even louder, symphony of horns.

By the time he reached the other side of the street, Chandler estimated that he had gained perhaps twenty yards on the fleeing boy and girl. Now it was a straight foot race, and he knew he was about to find out how well determination and anger in a thirty-year-old matched up against the legs and lungs of a couple at least a decade younger. At the moment, Chandler thought, he did not think he was going to make out too well; fifty yards ahead of him, the couple circled a fruit stand, ducked into another alley to their right.

Determination and anger won out; Chandler found them halfway up the alley, sitting on overturned garbage cans with their heads down and chests heaving as they gasped for breath. Chandler staggered the last fifteen yards, sat down next to Mary Beth Hart on her garbage can and panted along with them.

The young man was the first to speak. "This is a bad trip, man," he gasped to Chandler, then picked up a garbage can cover in a gesture that would have seemed menacing if he hadn't looked about ready to topple off the can he was sitting on. "Leave the girl alone; she has a right to do what she wants."

Chandler looked up. Just above and behind the young man's head, close to a dozen faded, yellowing posters of missing children had been taped to the grimy, soot-blackened brick wall. The tattered edges of the posters fluttered in the light breeze that blew down the alley, like sad banners left behind by a lost army.

"It's going to be a bad trip for you, sonny, if you don't put down that garbage can lid and split. This girl's under age. Is an easy piece of young ass worth getting your old ass thrown into the slammer?"

The young man swallowed nervously, licked his lips, glanced furtively at the girl. "I love her."

"Sure you do; that's why you let her strip for peepers instead of getting your own ass to work." Chandler took a quarter out of his pocket and flipped it to the young man, who reflexively reached out with one hand and caught it. "Go get yourself a job, sonny, and use that quarter to call Mary Beth in three or four years. Now put down that lid and get the hell out of here, or I'm going to punch your fucking lights out."

The young man hesitated, then abruptly dropped his weapon, rose to his feet and quickly walked away.

"You can take me back to my parents," the girl said, her mouth drawn down in a pout as she stared after the departing figure, "but you can't make me like it."

"It's not my job to make you like it," Chandler said as he grasped one of the posters of Cheryl Mosely he still carried under his arm and held it up for the girl to look at. "You know this one? You ever see her on the streets or working in the peep shows?"

The girl shook her head. Chandler sighed, rose and walked across the alley to the opposite wall with its rippling, small sea of small paper faces. He found a few pieces of tape that were still sticky, used them to tape up the poster of Cheryl Mosely.

"So?" Mary Beth Hart's voice was soft and sad now, almost a plea. "When are we going?"

Chandler turned, smiled gently at Mary Beth Hart and held out his hand. The girl rose, grasped Chandler's hand tightly, and together they walked toward the bright pillar of sunlight at the end of the alley.

A half hour after taking Mary Beth Hart back to her parents, Chandler was back on the streets, working the sex shops, juice bars and video arcades, nailing up more posters. He was coming out of a peep show on Melrose when an L.A.P.D. squad car pulled up to the curb, and a woman police officer leaned out the window. Chandler smiled and started to wave when he saw the familiar face of Jane Lincoln, who with her partner worked the missing children beat. His hand froze in mid-air when he saw the expression on the woman's face.

"The Lieutenant said we'd probably find you around

here, Chandler," Jane Lincoln said quietly. "He thought you might want to be in on this. Feel like taking a ride out to Studio City?"

"What'd you find?" Chandler asked dejectedly as he got into the back seat of the squad car, leaned his head back and sighed.

"We think Cheryl Mosely."

Cheryl Mosely's naked body, which looked as if it had been completely drained of blood, lay bleached-bone white in the tall, brown grass. The hillside was thirty yards above a frame house that was white with blue shutters, relatively isolated from the other houses in the neighborhood. Someone had cut open the girl's throat with a jagged-edged instrument; the serrated edges of the flaps of skin on each side of the gaping wound resembled nothing so much as an open, blood-red shark's mouth.

"That her, Jarrell?"

Chandler, feeling short of breath and distinctly nauseous, looked up at the man who had spoken. Although the hillside was in late-afternoon shadow, Lieutenant Ashley Boggs's hat was tilted low over his forehead, as if to shield his eyes not from light, but from evil. His mouth was set in a firm line, and he was indulging in his unconscious habit of frequently, softly, sighing, as if in despair at the present fate of Cheryl Mosely, and others like her in the past and future. He was a good man, Chandler thought; Ashley Boggs had been at his job a long time, and hadn't yet grown calloused.

"Yeah," Chandler said quietly. "It's Cheryl Mosely. Thanks for bringing me over, Boggs."

"You're thanking me for giving you the opportunity to look at this?"

"An end is an end, and it saves time when you find out you've reached it."

"How long was she missing?"

"A little less than a month. Have you notified the parents?"

Boggs shook his head. "We wanted a positive I.D. first."

"You've got it. I'll tell them."

"Okay." The police lieutenant paused, aimed his thumb and forefinger like a gun down the hillside in the direction of the white frame house. "You want to see the rest?"

"Not really, but I may as well since I'm here. The parents may want to know."

"Be my guest," Boggs said, moving to his left where railroad ties set into the hillside served as steps leading down to the house.

"Just a minute, Lieutenant. Can I move her?"

Boggs shook his head. "Forensic and the photographers want to come back and do some more work on the scene. You're a straight-arrow P.I., so I don't mind giving you a little preferential treatment when we come up with something that involves one of your clients, but we're still right in the middle of things here. Look all you want, but don't touch anything."

Taking care not to disturb the body and to stay on the wooden planks the police had set up around the scene, Chandler, bending over, slowly walked around the corpse. He stopped when he came to the left shoulder, got down on his hands and knees and peered even closer.

On the parchment flesh of the girl's left shoulder, almost hidden by the tall grass, was a small, brilliantly colored tattoo of a yellow dragon. The tattoo was so fresh that the needle marks were still plainly evident, like dozens of tiny angry insect bites, inside the garish yellow of the dragon. Chandler straightened up, started down the railroad-tie steps after the policeman.

"Got anything?" Chandler asked.

"Not a whole hell of a lot," Boggs replied over his shoulder. "The owner of the house lives in Malibu, rents it out. Three days ago, according to a neighbor, the rental sign goes down and a white truck—a big van—backs over the front lawn, right up to the door."

"A whole, white truckful of shy tenants," Chandler said with a sharp, bitter laugh.

"Or contraband—but if they were processing drugs, they did a good job of cleaning up after themselves."

"Who rented the place?"

"The girl did—by phone. Paid with cash."

"Anybody get the plates on the truck?"

"Nope. Anyway, right off the neighbors start hearing some strange shit coming from the house."

"What sort of 'strange shit'?"

"They describe it as a low hum, or a murmur; maybe singing."

It was ridiculous, Chandler thought; he was having to fight back tears. "Maybe it was the Mormon Tabernacle Choir."

"Yeah—but if that's who it was, they had a short rehearsal. Ten o'clock last night the white van pulls up again, and the murmuring stops. A neighbor found the body this morning when he came out to walk his dog."

Chandler reached the back of the house, entered the kitchen through a door Boggs held open for him. Following police markings on the floor, he walked

33

down a short, narrow hallway, turned right into the living room—and stopped so abruptly that Boggs bumped into him.

All four walls of the room were covered with freshly painted, blood red, arcane symbols—circles, crescents, whorls and dots, all interconnected by bars and squiggles of various widths.

"What's the matter, Jarrell? You sick?"

"No."

"You sure? You look like hell."

"I'm sure."

"You read Sanskrit?"

"Is that what it is?"

"According to one of our bright young college grads in forensics, that's what it is."

"No, I don't read Sanskrit."

"It mean something to you?"

"No," Chandler said, and tore his gaze away from the strange writing on the walls. He looked down at the floor, where he saw a strange pattern of depressions in the carpet, in the center of the room. Careful to keep his eyes off the walls, he moved closer, bent down to examine the marks. Twelve lines, perhaps two inches wide and four feet long, radiated from a circle perhaps a foot and a half in diameter. "What the hell made that?"

"Beats us," Boggs replied evenly. "Maybe a weird coffee table."

"It would have to be one hell of a heavy coffee table to make marks that deep in so short a time."

"Right."

Chandler straightened up and, taking care not to step on the impressions, went back out into the hallway, where he would not see the strange, ominous markings that filled him with so much dread.

"I referred somebody to you the other day," Boggs continued quietly as he followed Chandler out of the room.

"I know. Thanks."

"You take the case?"

"No," Chandler replied curtly, still shaken by the blood, the markings, the dead girl. Fearing that his distress was reflected on his face, he turned his back to the other man.

"Easy job, Jarrell."

"Yeah. It sounded that way."

"You've been in the P.I. business for five years, and you still only take the missing kid cases, huh?"

"Yeah."

"You should have stayed a social worker, Jarrell," Boggs said, not unkindly. "At least you could count on a steady paycheck."

"I like being self-employed."

"Is *that* what they're calling poverty these days? How much can you make on these kid cases?"

"None of your business, Lieutenant."

"Small change, right? What are the Moselys paying you? And no matter how much or how little they gave you up front, how much are they going to pay you now for finding them a dead daughter?"

"Lieutenant, that's none of your business, either. You mind if I look in the other rooms?"

"Go ahead, just don't touch anything."

Chandler walked down the hallway to the front of the house, turned left and entered a small area he suspected had once been used as a music or sewing room.

The room was bare, with no markings on the walls or the bare wood floor. The last rays of the setting sun were slanting in through a large, dirt-streaked picture window, filling the room with a kind of striped, burnished glow. Chandler went to the window, looked out—and started.

It seemed incredible to Chandler that the Oriental woman would have gone to the trouble of following him around since just before noontime, and yet that was obviously what she had done. The front lawn of the house was marked off by yellow police tape, but up and down both sides of the street neighbors had gathered in little knots to talk excitedly and occasionally gesture toward the house. Down the street, to Chandler's right, Kee Nang stood talking quietly with an elderly Oriental man who appeared to be a gardener. The man pointed to the house; the woman turned, and her gaze locked with Chandler's. Chandler stared back at Kee Nang for a few moments, then shook his head in dismay before turning away from the window and walking out of the room. He went back through the house, past the living room where Ashley Boggs was talking to a police photographer, into the kitchen to wait until one of the police officers had time to take him home.

On the stove was a pot of oatmeal, looking decidedly incongruous in the otherwise bare kitchen. Chandler went over to the range, looked down at the cold, lumpy mess, and frowned. There was something not right . . .

Although he knew he shouldn't, Chandler reached down with his index finger and pushed at the congealed skin on the surface of the oatmeal; the skin stretched, but did not give. Chandler put his finger at the juncture between the skin and the edge of the battered metal pot, and pushed harder. This time the thick skin parted from the side of the pot, and Chandler uttered a sharp cry, snatching his stained finger away and watching with a mounting sense of astonishment and horror as the depression in the oatmeal slowly filled with a viscous, dark red fluid that was unmistakably blood.

Chapter Four

CHANDLER, SHOULDERS HUNCHED INSIDE HIS LIGHT JACK-
et against the cold rain that fell from a slate sky, stood
away from the others as the final prayer was said. A
shovelful of dirt was spilled over the white coffin, and
the small family gathering began to break up. Chandler
turned and walked back toward the winding cemetery
drive, waited just beyond a grove of pines as the
Moselys, a middle-aged couple whose shoulders were
stooped with sorrow, came down the walk.

"I'm so sorry," Chandler said as he fell into step
beside the woman.

The man heaved a deep, shuddering sigh. "Well, I
guess that's the end of that." He paused, glanced at
Chandler with red-rimmed eyes that reflected more
than a hint of hostility. "I owe you money, Jarrell?"

Chandler stiffened, caught himself as he was about to glance over his shoulder at the fresh grave on a hill in the field of grave markers behind them. "I'll send you a bill," he said tersely.

"Oh, I'm sure you will," the man said curtly as he released his grip on his wife's arm and walked quickly away.

The woman started to hurry after her husband, then abruptly stopped, turned and walked back to where Chandler was standing. "I apologize, Mr. Jarrell."

"There's nothing for you to apologize for. I've intruded."

The slight woman shook her head, gazed intently at Chandler with eyes that seemed unnaturally green in the rainy light. She reached up with a trembling hand and brushed a soaked strand of hair back from her forehead. "My husband doesn't mean to be rude. He knows, like I do, that you did everything you could to find Cheryl before . . . He loved Cheryl so much. He had . . . such high expectations for her. I suppose Cheryl tried as best she could, but—"

"Mrs. Mosely," Chandler interrupted, taking the woman by the elbow, "let's get you out of the rain."

The woman, showing physical strength that surprised Chandler, didn't move, and Chandler removed his hand from her elbow. "Mr. Jarrell," she said, raising her face to him and thrusting out her chin, "I want you to find the people who killed Cheryl."

Chandler watched rain drip off the woman's chin, to fall and quickly disappear like the dreams of her daughter in the water swirling at their feet. "Mrs. Mosely, I don't think—"

"Please, Mr. Jarrell," the woman said as she quickly fumbled in her purse. She brought out a roll of bills tightly wrapped in a rubber band, held it out to him. "I brought this with me because I was hoping you'd be here. It's three hundred and twenty-six dollars: it's mine—I earned it myself, so it doesn't have anything to do with my husband. Please take it. I want you to find Cheryl's killer."

Chandler moved closer to the woman, trying to shield her as best he could from the rain. "Mrs. Mosely," he said gently, "I can understand how you feel, but the police will be doing that."

"Mr. Jarrell, look me right in the eye and tell me you think the police are going to find whoever it was that killed Cheryl."

Chandler met the woman's gaze, but remained silent; there was nothing to say, for he knew the terrible odds against justice in this case. There were just too many broken and breaking children like Cheryl Mosely in Los Angeles.

"So," the woman continued with a bitter sigh. "Take the money, Mr. Jarrell."

"We can talk another time, ma'am."

The woman's green eyes flashed. Water dripped off flesh and paper as the frail hand holding the money remained firmly outstretched. "Look, it's my daughter buried back there, so I figure that gives me the right to decide whether or not this is the proper time and place to discuss the business of finding her murderer."

Chandler looked at the money, then into the woman's face. "Ma'am, did Cheryl have a tattoo before she left home?"

The woman blinked with surprise, and the hand with the money slowly dropped to her side. "Good heavens, no," she said, clearly startled.

"Are you sure? This tattoo would be on her left

shoulder. Maybe she had it done without you or your husband knowing about it, and she hid it from you."

"I'm positive," the woman replied in a firm voice. "Cheryl had no tattoo when she left home—not on her left shoulder, nor anywhere else. Will you please take the money? It will make me feel much better if I can leave this terrible place knowing that we have an agreement and that you'll be looking for Cheryl's killer."

"Mrs. Mosely," Chandler said with a sigh and a slight shake of his head, "I don't have any experience with murder investigations."

"I don't care." Once again the woman held out the rain-soaked wad of money. "I want you."

"I'll look into it, Mrs. Mosely, see if there's anything I might be able to do that the police can't. If there is, then we can talk about how much—"

"Thank you very much, Mr. Jarrell," the woman said as she stepped forward, reached inside Chandler's jacket and firmly stuffed the roll of bills into his shirt pocket. "Now I feel better."

Chandler stood in the rain, watching the black-draped woman walk quickly up the path to the drive, where her husband was waiting for her in the car. The man opened the door from inside; the woman got in, the door slammed shut, and the car pulled away.

The roll of money in Chandler's pocket felt like a dagger pressing against his heart.

The chicken pot pie he'd prepared for dinner reminded him too much of the blood-veined oatmeal, and Chandler tossed it into the garbage can without eating any. He poured himself a beer, took a hunk of cheese out of the refrigerator, then went to the kitchen window and ate as he stared out into the rain and wind-swept darkness.

He'd meant to get back to work on the streets after the funeral—but he'd been exhausted, and he'd ended by coming home. He now had not only Cheryl Mosely's killer to search for, but a half-dozen other missing children for whom an hour lost could mean another shot of dope, another trick, a lifetime. He'd meant to take a nap, then go out when he felt more rested. But he hadn't been able to sleep, or to arouse enough energy to leave the house. He felt as if his mind and body were filled with stale air that was sapping his strength and will. Too many dead or broken kids, he thought. And now the symbols on the walls of the house where Cheryl Mosely had been slaughtered, symbols that meant another puzzle to crack.

Outside his window, the eucalyptus grove to his right was a crowd of dark, ominous, twisted shapes in the darkness. Down the hill that was the back lawn of his Silver Lake home, on an otherwise empty street, a new Buick sat parked beneath a streetlamp, where it had been standing all day. Now, as during the dark day, it was impossible to see clearly into the car's interior through the rain-streaked windows, but in the glow of the streetlamp it seemed to Chandler that—sometimes —he could just make out the dark, blobby shape of a person inside the car.

He felt better when he'd eaten the cheese and drunk the beer. He took a red felt marker out of a kitchen drawer, then went into his small study between the kitchen and living room. Two walls of the study were lined with bookshelves, and a full trophy case attested to his athletic prowess in high school and college. There were a number of framed certificates of commendation from the Los Angeles Social Services Bureau and the Los Angeles Police Department.

He removed the Los Angeles telephone directory from a shelf, sat down at his desk and quickly turned to the classified section. He flipped through to the T's, stopped when he came to the listings for tattoo parlors. There were five. He circled them with the marker, then tore out the page and placed it under a paperweight on his desk. He put the directory back on the shelf, rose and stretched. It was the first work he'd done all day, he thought with a thin smile, and he decided to reward himself for his labors with a second can of beer, and maybe even make himself a sandwich; the cheese had whetted his appetite.

The Buick was still parked beneath the streetlamp when he went back to the kitchen window; as lightning flashed across the sky and created a kind of stroboscopic effect on the landscape below, he definitely saw the outline of someone sitting behind the wheel of the car.

There was no reason for anyone to sit in a parked car for hours in the rain below his house, Chandler thought. Not unless they were watching him.

He put his half-eaten sandwich down on the counter next to his beer, then went to the darkened front of the house and took a black slicker out of a hall closet. He slipped out the front door, ran through the rain up the block, then cut across a neighbor's back lawn to the hillside. Keeping low, he slipped and slid down the slick hillside to the street, a hundred yards above the car. He sprinted down the street, snatched open the door on the driver's side.

"All right, pal!" Chandler shouted. "What the hell are you—?!"

There was no one behind the wheel of the Buick.

44

Chandler put his head into the car, looked into the back: the car was empty. He backed out of the car, looked up and down the street. There was no one in sight.

Chandler stood in the pouring rain on the deserted street for almost fifteen minutes before finally working up the resolve to climb back up the hillside to his house. Suddenly he was very tired . . .

If only he could get a decent night's sleep . . .

Twenty feet above the ground, perched delicately on the crossbeam of a streetlamp where she had leaped at Chandler's approach, Kee Nang watched, her heart filled with a mixture of fear, sorrow and resolve as Chandler trudged wearily back up the hillside to his house and disappeared inside. Then, with skills, reflexes and balance born of a lifetime of martial arts training, she dropped down to the street, just outside the pool of yellow light cast by the streetlamp. She landed lightly on the balls of her feet, flexing her knees and bouncing once to absorb the shock of her landing.

"Sleep well, Chosen One," she murmured, once more glancing up at the house as she got back into her car. "You will need your rest—and all of your strength."

Chapter Five

THE SEVEN STAR TRADING COMPANY WAREHOUSE STOOD by itself at the end of a potholed, lonely, deteriorating street lined on both sides by factories, warehouses and empty lots surrounded by chain-link fences, near Long Beach Harbor.

Atop the warehouse, his grotesque shape silhouetted against a full moon, the monkey man sat in silent vigil.

Inside, stationed against the four walls which were marked with crimson symbols of evil, four naked, perspiring men with glazed eyes sat in the lotus position. The incessant, low chanting of the hypnotized men was dissonant and grating, reverberating in sonic waves of evil throughout the vast, nearly empty chamber. Anti-prayers; barriers against good.

In the center of the room, the golden child, awash in a dull bronze glow, sat inside the twelve-armed cage, unconcernedly staring back at the giant Til, who was growing increasingly puzzled and frustrated by the bizarre and potentially deadly game he had chosen to play.

Once again, as he had been doing for close to an hour, Til selected a stone from the diminishing pile in front of him, loaded it into the slingshot he held, and let the missile fly at the child's head. Once again, the child merely nodded his head; the stone veered away, flying harmlessly past the cage and striking the far wall, narrowly missing one of the glassy-eyed chanters.

The giant picked up another stone, loaded it into his slingshot and fired. The result was the same.

Til snorted, picked up yet another stone and casually tossed it toward the cage. This time the child moved his right hand; the stone veered off at a much sharper angle, shot up into the air and danced in a light, quick circuit around one of the bare lightbulbs suspended from the ceiling.

This was a new, startling twist to the game, and Til sat up straight and stared in astonishment, first at the ceiling, and then in wonder at the child. The boy merely stared back impassively.

Til tossed another stone. The boy moved his hand in the opposite direction; the stone shot up to the ceiling, and skipped across it as though skimming over water.

Man and boy stared at each other—and suddenly the boy's face was wreathed with a smile.

"Ha!" Til shouted as he snatched up the largest stone in the pile, loaded it into his slingshot and let it fly at the boy's head. He had hoped to catch the child by surprise, but the boy merely raised his hand—this time with the palm facing outward. Til barely had time to duck as the large stone came flying back at him and smashed against the wall where he was sitting.

Til, beads of perspiration forming around the callus on his forehead, gaped in amazement at the child—who suddenly began to laugh.

Then Til laughed. It was time for a new game, he thought, one that was not so dangerous for *him*. He looked around him, then rose and walked over to a soda machine set against the wall a few yards away. He picked up the trash basket next to the machine and carried it out into the center of the room, setting it down a few feet from the cage. He took an aluminum can out of the basket, stepped back a few paces and tossed the can easily toward the cage.

The golden child raised a hand; the can spun around in the air, reversed direction, landed in the basket—and popped out again to rattle on the floor at the giant's feet.

"Ha!" Til cried in astonishment and delight. He picked up the can and tossed it again. Again, the can spun, landed in the basket, popped out and landed at the giant's feet.

On the fourth toss, the can landed a few feet away. Til started to walk toward it, then stopped and uttered a startled cry as the can started to spin. Til's eyes went wide as the can imploded, twisted, expanded, imploded again, finally reshaping itself as a little tin man which jumped up and began to dance a jig.

Both child and man laughed with delight, and soon Til was clapping a rhythm and jumping about in a lumbering imitation of the little dancing tin man. He continued to laugh, dance and clap for almost a minute —then cried out in shock and terror when Sardo

Numspa suddenly appeared from nowhere to crush the little tin man under his booted foot.

"Get that out of here!" the dark-eyed man shouted in a booming voice, pointing a trembling finger at the trash basket, then at the vending machine. "Get everything out of here!"

As Til hurried to obey, Numspa produced a bowl of oatmeal from inside the folds of his coat, bent down and set it in front of the cage. He glared at the boy, who gazed steadily, bravely, back at him.

"You will eat!" Numspa shouted. "You *must* eat!"

And then Sardo Numspa was gone, disappearing in a ripple of brown light.

The golden child stared at the bowl of oatmeal for some time, then slowly reached out and tipped it over; blood-streaked oatmeal oozed out over the grease-stained concrete floor. The child reached inside his robe and withdrew a small twig on which there were four leaves. He closed his eyes in silent prayer for a few moments, then plucked a leaf from the twig, put it in his mouth and slowly, thoughtfully, began to chew. He returned the twig with its three remaining leaves to the folds of his robe, and continued to chew until the leaf was gone. Then, amid the incessant, evil chanting, the golden child sat, his gaze on the far wall and his face impassive, patiently waiting . . .

Chapter Six

STRIKE FIVE.

So much for tattoo parlors, Chandler thought as he tossed the page he had torn from his directory into a wire trash basket outside the fifth, and last, tattoo parlor listed. No one had tattooed a yellow dragon onto the left shoulder of a young girl recently; no one he'd talked to had *ever* tattooed a yellow dragon on anyone. They didn't do yellow dragons, he'd been told; green dragons, yes, and even an occasional black dragon, but not yellow.

He was tired, irritable, anxious. Depressed. All night he had dreamed of seven stars which glowed with a sickly red light; just beyond the light, terrible things had moved; twisted, poisonous creatures lurking, waiting—for him?

And there had been the chanting, an evil sound

which had seemed to stay in his mind even after he had awoken.

He wondered if he was losing his mind.

He'd wasted the better part of the morning and three-quarters of a tank of gas, Chandler thought, on a wild yellow dragon hunt. Just so the morning wouldn't be a total waste, he decided he would confront, and get rid of, his tail. Although the Buick parked on the street outside his house had been gone in the morning, he'd felt the woman's presence at his back from the time he'd left the house and started making the rounds of the tattoo parlors. That presence was starting to annoy him, and he figured he might just as well take out some of his anger and frustration on this particular Los Angeles loony as on anyone else.

He abruptly stopped walking and wheeled around. Except for three teenagers leaning against the gleaming hood of a Mercedes, the sidewalk was empty. The woman who called herself Kee Nang was quick, Chandler thought—but she was damn well around someplace, and he suddenly found himself even more irritated by the fact that she was prompting him into playing hide and seek. It was enough that talking with her brought him bad dreams at night; he didn't need her following him around during the day.

Chandler quickly walked back the way he had come, glancing from left to right into storefronts and alleys on both sides of the street. There was no sign of Kee Nang. He passed the dark mouth of yet another alley—and abruptly stopped.

Chandler turned to face the darkness, put his hands on his hips. "All right, lady, you've been following me all day," he said curtly. "So here I am. Now come on out."

Kee Nang's soft voice came from just behind his left ear. "I am out."

"Jesus *Christ!*" Chandler yelped, thoroughly startled. He spun around, found Kee Nang standing just inches from him. She was dressed in an outfit almost identical to the one in which Chandler had first seen her, except that she now wore a white jersey instead of a blue blouse. "Where the hell did you just come from?!"

Kee Nang smiled slightly, shrugged, then lifted her arms and gestured to indicate the empty street around them. "You told me to come out, Mr. Jarrell."

"You've been following me!"

"Have I?"

"Yes, damn it! Why?"

"Perhaps to protect you."

"From what?"

"Evil," Kee Nang answered simply.

"I don't need your protection, lady; I probably need protection *from* you. It was you sitting in the Buick in front of my house yesterday, wasn't it?"

"Was it?"

"Damn straight."

Kee Nang cocked her head to one side, smiled quizzically. "How can you be so sure?"

Chandler frowned; he was puzzled by his certainty, but it was nonetheless there. "I'm just sure. Why were you down there?"

"Perhaps to protect you from evil."

"Yeah? Well, what would have happened if evil had pounced on me while you were out to lunch?"

"Excuse me? I don't understand."

"Where did you go? When I came down looking for you, you weren't in the car."

"I must have gone for a walk."

"In the rain?"

"Pardon me, Mr. Jarrell, but now I'm confused. First you seemed upset because you were convinced I'd been sitting in a car by your house; now you seem upset because you didn't find me in the car. Which is it?"

"What are you, a goddam lawyer?!" Chandler snapped, and immediately felt foolish. As a result, he said something else which made him feel even more foolish. "It's not going to help you to follow me around; I'm not going to take your case."

"You are already on it. I've told you it is your destiny; you cannot avoid it. You can die, or worse— which is something I must try to prevent—but you cannot avoid searching for the child."

"You're full of—" Chandler bit off the bitter words, turned and started to walk away. "Leave me alone."

"Mr. Jarrell," the woman said in a voice that was very soft but nonetheless easily reached Chandler, startled him and made him stop so fast he almost stumbled, "the Golden Child was held in the house where the girl—Cheryl Mosely—was killed." Chandler slowly turned back to face the woman; Kee Nang was once more standing only inches from him, although he had not heard her walk up behind him. She continued, "Now do I have your attention?"

Chandler sat stiffly in the booth in the coffee shop, a chill spreading through him as he watched the woman quickly draw on a paper napkin, in perfect detail, the symbols he had seen on the walls of the killing-house— and in his dreams. Kee Nang finished, pushed the napkin across the table to him; Chandler set his glass of iced tea down on it.

"How did you get Lieutenant Boggs to let you in the house?" he asked.

"I was not in the house."

"Then how do you know about this?" Chandler asked tersely, tapping his glass on the napkin. For a moment it had occurred to him that the woman might have been involved in the killing; he had almost immediately dismissed the notion—although he was not certain why. Maybe, he thought with a feeling of bittersweet irony which he was careful not to let show on his face, it was the way she looked; Kee Nang simply looked innocent.

"I know."

"What is it?"

"Tibetan writing."

"I was told it's Sanskrit."

"It is Tibetan."

"What does it mean?"

"It is a restraint curse. The people who have taken the *Gompen Tarma* must restrain him spiritually as well as physically. To do that, they must keep evil on all four sides of him. However, the writing alone would not be enough; they would have to augment it with something else."

Chandler felt his stomach muscles tighten, then begin to flutter. "Like chanting?"

"Yes," Kee Nang said, suddenly looking at him strangely. "The chanting of evil prayers, combined with the restraint curse, would effectively imprison him. What made you say that?"

"Nothing," Chandler said quickly—too quickly, he knew. He was afraid. He'd seen plenty of crazy people in his past life, which had ended five years before. He'd served clients recently released from mental institutions, had seen what the experience—and their minds —had done to them. He did not want to be crazy himself. "It was just a guess. What happens if they don't keep the kid's, uh, spirit locked up tight?"

"The *Gompen Tarma* might project himself astrally."

"You mean, he might show up in my living room?"

"Perhaps," the woman replied evenly.

"I don't believe that," Chandler said in a flat tone.

"It would not matter, if someone dropped a heavy object on your head, whether you believe in gravity or not. It does not matter whether you believe that the Golden Child can project astrally. He can."

"Gravity and astral projection aren't the same thing. One is scientific, the other is superstition. Magic."

"Is television magic?"

"Of course not," Chandler replied tersely, already feeling defensive and not liking it.

"Try telling that to some New Guinea native whose only means of long-distance communication is the beating of a drum or a hollow log. Just because something is beyond your capacity to understand, or is outside your immediate experience, doesn't make it superstition."

Chandler swallowed hard. "What does it say?" he asked, again tapping his glass on the napkin.

"Why won't you look at the writing?"

"I've already seen it, and I wouldn't want to leave watermarks on this beautiful Formica tabletop. What does it say?"

"The world is wicked. Let it perish."

"Not all that bad a thought," Chandler said, surprised by the unexpected bitterness that had suddenly, without warning, surfaced in his heart, and which he heard in his voice.

Kee Nang studied him with her large, soulful black eyes. "You don't see much good in the world, do you?"

"Not much. And I've done a lot of looking around, seen a lot of bad things."

"I believe you," Kee Nang said softly. "You are a wounded man."

Not as wounded as he used to be, Chandler thought. And certainly not as wounded as some of the many people he had once tried, and failed, to help. It was what had made him finally leave a job in which he'd come to feel like a blind, crippled surgeon in an infinitely large, chaotic emergency room filled with the silent screams of helpless men, women and children. He had wanted to work in a much smaller arena where he could be effective, could truly help.

Some help he'd been to Cheryl Mosely, with her throat torn open by a human shark . . .

Chandler cleared his throat. "Do you believe that when—if—I find Cheryl Mosely's killer, I'll be finding the people who're holding your Gold—your kid?"

"Yes. That is what I have said."

"Do you know why Cheryl was killed?"

"No."

"I think I do." Suddenly, Chandler's mouth was very dry. He lifted his glass to drink some of the iced tea, and the napkin stuck to the bottom—the drawings Kee Nang had made were magnified and distorted by the glass, and Chandler quickly set it back down. "They may have wanted her blood—which they put in oatmeal they may have tried to feed to your kid. Why would they want to feed the kid blood?"

For the first time since he had met her, Chandler saw the woman lose her composure. Kee Nang's dark eyes were suddenly filled with alarm, and beads of perspiration appeared just below her gleaming black bangs. "You're sure of this?"

"I'm sure Cheryl Mosely's body was drained of blood; I'm sure there was a pot of oatmeal in the house, and I'm sure there was blood in it—a lot of blood."

Kee Nang, her face ashen and her eyes wide with fear, sat in silence for some time, staring off into the distance at what Chandler could sense was her own, private nightmare. Finally she rose from the table, put her hand out to him. "Come with me, Chandler. Please."

"I have work to do, Kee Nang."

"This is your work; there is someone we must talk to about the blood."

They rode in Chandler's old Ford station wagon, with Kee Nang giving directions in a small, frightened voice, to Chinatown, to a street that was little wider or longer than an alley. He parked the station wagon, got out and followed Kee Nang to an old, dilapidated building housing what appeared to be an herb shop. There had been no sound when Kee Nang had entered the shop, but when he passed through the door chimes tolled from somewhere deep inside the building. He found himself in a musky room filled with thousands of arcane objects, large and small, most of which were covered with a thick layer of dust. Along one wall was a glass display case containing at least a hundred different containers filled with powders of various colors and consistencies.

There was no one in the front of the shop, and Chandler followed Kee Nang through a thick curtain, down a dimly-lit corridor, and into a room on the left which smelled strongly of an incense that reminded Chandler of a forest in the rain. There were two old men in the room: one had a shaved head, and wore a long, flowing, orange robe; the other was toothless, and lay on a low couch, naked to the waist. Chandler blinked in surprise and shock when he saw smoke rising from the toothless man's back, but then realized that what was burning was not flesh, but a small mound of blue powder which had been placed between the man's shoulder blades.

Kee Nang whispered something in the ear of the man in the orange robe. The man turned, bowed slightly to Chandler.

"I am Dr. Hong, Mr. Jarrell," the old man said in perfect English, smiling. "You honor my shop with your presence. Welcome."

Chandler bowed in return to the man in the orange robe, then to the other old man, who had spoken to him in Chinese.

"He says he, too, is very pleased to meet a man as great as you," Dr. Hong continued, bowing again.

"Yeah," Chandler replied, and found that he was growing impatient. "You tell him I'm also honored. Look, Dr. Hong, Kee Nang seems to think that—"

"We must speak to Kala," Kee Nang interrupted.

Hong studied Kee Nang's drawn face, glanced at Chandler, then nodded gravely. "Follow me, please," he said, and ducked through a curtain at the rear of the room.

Chandler, with a growing sense of uneasiness, followed Kee Nang through the curtain and found himself in yet another long, narrow, dimly lit corridor. This corridor was decorated with paintings of various sizes depicting what appeared to be mythical Chinese beings, dragons and demons and—

Suddenly Chandler felt nauseous, short of breath and dizzy. His vision blurred, and it was only after a few moments that he realized he had stopped walking and was supporting himself by leaning with both hands against the wall. Before him, framed by his outstretched arms and only inches from his face, was the painting which had caused his disorientation—a depiction of some kind of creature with a crocodile's body and bat's wings. The wings, tipped with curving saber claws, were enormous, stretching back over its body and beyond into the darkness of the painting. The creature's face was that of a rodent, except for teeth which, like its claws, were long and curved, extending from both the top and bottom of its mouth. The huge, gaping eyes were red on red—pools of blood with flame-pupils burning in their centers. The expression on the creature's face reflected such malevolent and merciless cruelty that it made Chandler feel gutted and empty inside, hopelessly alone. Such a thing, if it existed, would allow nothing that was good to survive: it would not be able to tolerate goodness, beauty, love . . .

But it didn't exist, Chandler thought; such a thing couldn't exist except in nightmares.

Slowly, he became aware of the woman standing beside him; then he felt her gentle touch on his back.

"Chandler? What's the matter?"

"Nothing," Chandler said, but he continued to lean against the wall. "I must be allergic to incense. What's this beastie in the painting?"

"That is Sardo Numspa," Kee Nang said in an oddly flat tone of voice in which Chandler thought he detected a tremor of fear. "Sardo Numspa is a . . . very powerful demon. Why do you ask?"

"No reason at all," Chandler replied curtly, fighting off a second wave of dizziness as he pushed off the wall. "Ugly critter, isn't he?"

"Yes," Kee Nang said in the same flat voice. "He is also unspeakably evil."

"Well, as far as I'm concerned, when you've seen one demon, you've seen them all," Chandler said, gripping Kee Nang's elbow and guiding her down the corridor toward the curtain through which Dr. Hong had already disappeared. "Let's go."

At the end of the corridor, Kee Nang pulled the curtain aside, and Chandler passed into a room which was even darker than the corridor. He stopped and stood still for a few seconds, waiting for his eyes to become accustomed to the gloom.

Gradually he became aware of Hong's figure on the opposite side of the room, which Chandler now saw was quite large. A few moments later he became aware that Hong was standing at the foot of a raised platform which was veiled by another curtain—this one quite thin, like a theatrical scrim. Behind the scrim, faintly backlit by what Chandler assumed was a tiny candle, he could see the vague profile of a woman sitting sideways, naked from the waist up: he could see the clear outline of firm, large breasts and pointed nipples.

Just what he needed, Chandler thought as anger rose within him to mix with his nausea and dizziness, to waste an afternoon after a wasted morning by ending up in a tame Chinese peep show.

Except that sex wasn't what this was about at all, he thought, and felt his initial anger replaced by doubt. And fear. Kee Nang *had* precisely reproduced the

61

writing on the walls in the house where Cheryl Mosely had been killed. And she knew something about the bloody oatmeal. He had no choice but to listen.

"You may speak with Kala, Mr. Jarrell," Hong said quietly.

Chandler started to walk toward the scrim, but Kee Nang's hand suddenly gripped his elbow firmly, holding him back.

"Speak from there, Mr. Jarrell," the old man continued. "Kala will hear you."

"This isn't my show," Chandler said tersely, very conscious of the woman's incredibly strong grip on his arm. "I came to listen, not talk. Kee Nang brought me here: let her ask the questions."

"Kala will speak only to you," Hong said in the same soft voice.

"Why?"

"As Kee Nang has told you, you are the Chosen One. Kala will speak to no other on this matter."

"I don't know what questions to ask."

"You will find them."

"Okay, then—tell me about the missing kid, lady," Chandler said to the backlit, half-naked figure behind the scrim.

"Every thousand years a perfect child is born," the figure intoned. "It is the *Gompen Tarma,* the 'Golden Child.' This one is the fourth; he has come to rescue us."

Chandler blinked, and would have taken a step backward if it were not for Kee Nang's iron grip on his arm holding him in place. The voice was eerie and rasping, not at all like that of a young woman—which the figure appeared to be—but like that of an old man, or an old . . . something.

"Rescue us from what?" he asked tightly.

"From ourselves," the rasping voice replied. "The Golden Child is the bringer of compassion. If he dies, compassion will die with him."

"This is some kind of religious gig, isn't it? You the leader of this sect, lady? What do you call yourselves?"

"This has nothing to do with religions, Mr. Jarrell, I assure you."

"I need to know just what this gig is, lady; it will help. What's the name of your organization?"

"I repeat: This has nothing to do with religions."

"But you're saying that without the kid, the world will go to hell. Right?"

"Hell?"

"Yeah; you know, *hell*."

"This song will no longer be sung."

"Come again?"

"The world will become hell, as I believe you imagine hell to be. The answer to your question is, yes."

"That's religion."

"Hell, as you call it, has nothing to do with religion. Many of the thousands of humankind's religions have presumed to try to *describe* this plane of existence, but the plane exists independently of religions or their feeble descriptions. Do not confuse an actual abyss with a painter's rendering of an abyss. Religions paint pictures."

"I don't believe in hell, lady."

"That is of no consequence: it remains."

"Who do you think took the kid?"

"Those who want evil rather than good."

Chandler sighed. "I don't suppose you could be a bit more specific?"

"No. We do not know who took him."

"Why would they try to make him eat blood?"

For the first time, there was no immediate, rasping response from the figure behind the scrim. Almost a minute went by, then: "Is that what they are trying to do, Mr. Jarrell?"

"It's a possibility."

"Where did this blood come from?"

"I think a slaughtered girl."

"A sacrifice; then it is impure. Nothing in this song—this world—will hurt him; the smallest pebble will not strike him; the hottest fire will not burn him. But if he were to pollute himself with anything impure, he would become vulnerable."

"You're saying that as long as he doesn't eat the blood, nothing can harm him?"

"That is correct, Mr. Jarrell—as far as this song is concerned. But there are things in other songs that could—"

"Whoa, lady; hang on a second. Are we talking about a kidnapping or a concert? What's this 'song' business?"

"Forgive me, Mr. Jarrell; that is just a manner of speaking. What I mean is that there are things which are not of this world that can harm the *Gompen Tarma.*" There was another pause, this one lasting only a few seconds. "Do you have any other questions?"

"Jehovah's Witnesses, right?"

"What?" Suddenly, the voice seemed even more rasping.

"The business about the blood making him impure; this is some kind of kinky, Oriental offshoot of the Jehovah's Witnesses. Right? Look, I don't care what you are, or what you believe—but if you just wanted someone to help you set up some kind of publicity stunt, why the hell did you have to pick on me? I've got a few thousand more important things to—"

Chandler abruptly stopped speaking when he became aware of a rustling sound that seemed to come from nowhere and everywhere, filling the room. It reminded him of dry leaves, and he assumed that the woman behind the scrim had begun shaking some kind of ceremonial rattle. But her arms remained perfectly still at her sides.

The figure's voice, when it came, was as hard and dry as the rattling.

"*This* is the Chosen One?!"

It was the old man who answered, with just a trace of irony and regret in his voice. "Yes."

There was a prolonged silence, then: "Strange are the ways of destiny."

"Indeed," Dr. Hong said as Chandler tore his elbow free from Kee Nang's grip, wheeled around and strode quickly out of the room.

Chapter Seven

"Chandler! Please wait!"

Chandler didn't slow his pace, and he refused to look at Kee Nang when she finally caught up with him. Perhaps, he thought, it was not true that he had to follow this lead. Perhaps he should leave this madness behind, and fight anyone who seemed to be a part of it—or causing it.

"Chandler, what's the matter?!"

"You people certainly put on a good show," he said curtly as he turned a corner and headed at a fast pace down the block to where he had parked the car.

"Show?"

"Where did you get her from?"

"Kala? Kala is the librarian of the secret repository at Palkor Sin, Chandler. She was flown here to help us. She is over three hundred years old."

"My compliments to her plastic surgeon. From what I could see, she's a hell of a good-looking broad for her age. How does she manage it?"

"One of her ancestors was raped by a dragon."

Chandler's laugh was bitter, without humor. "No shit? A dragon, you say? I love it. That kind of thing happen a lot where you come from?"

"You asked me a question, Chandler, and I answered it. Were you just going to drive away and leave me here?"

"I figured somebody in that little shop of horrors back there would have an extra broomstick you could borrow."

"What?"

"I'm telling you to get lost, lady. Get out of my life."

Chandler reached the car, gripped the door handle and stopped, suddenly conscious of the fact that Kee Nang was no longer beside him. Abruptly, inexplicably, he felt a terrible sense of loss. He looked back, was relieved to find that she was standing a few yards away.

"Night is here, Chandler," the woman said softly. "Taxis do not like to come down here, and I am a long way from home. May I come with you, please?"

"This is fine," Kee Nang said when they had reached the street where Chandler had confronted her earlier in the day.

They were the first words either had spoken in the half-hour it had taken to drive up from Chinatown, and Chandler was vaguely surprised to discover how much he enjoyed hearing her voice. He turned in his seat, stared into the dark eyes. When he first saw her, he remembered, she had seemed plain to him. No longer. He wondered if this woman's extraordinary beauty, which he was only now beginning to appreciate, was something that worked subtly on the senses.

"I don't want to let you out in the middle of the street," Chandler said. "Tell me where you live, and I'll take you to the door."

"This will be fine, Chandler."

He turned back and faced straight ahead, looking through the windshield.

"Kee Nang, I'm sorry about the way I behaved back there. I wouldn't have driven away without you. I was just . . . pissed."

"What were you 'just pissed' about? Did somebody say something to offend you?"

"No. Like I said, I was just pissed. I can't explain why."

"The painting of Sardo Numspa upset you, didn't it?" Kee Nang asked, a new tension in her voice.

"No," Chandler replied tersely, quickly looking away. "Why should a picture of some dumb beastie upset me?"

"That is what I am asking. I know that it did."

"I said it didn't upset me," Chandler replied, gripping the wheel. Outside his window, two teenage prostitutes in hot pants, spike heels and tight tube tops, stopped on the sidewalk, bent over and peered into the car. They saw Kee Nang, sniffed contemptuously at what they obviously considered competition, walked stiffly on.

"Chandler," the woman said softly, reaching out and gently touching his arm, "please promise me that, no matter what you're thinking or what you believe right now, you'll do your best to save the Golden Child."

"I thought you said it was my destiny to find the kid, whether I wanted to or not," Chandler said tightly, following the young hookers with his eyes until they disappeared around a corner.

"Sometimes men and women turn their backs on their destinies. To have a destiny doesn't mean that one is not free. Because the tide of fate pushes you in a certain direction does not mean that you cannot try to swim against it—even if you must drown by doing so. If you try to swim against this tide, Chandler, the world will drown along with you. Promise me you will do your best."

"Sorry," Chandler said curtly. "I don't make promises."

"Why is that?"

The woman's touch, so gentle and yet so compelling, in itself felt like a tide—pulling him inexorably to her. It was a force he must fight . . .

"Because I might not be able to keep them."

"Why do you do this? Find lost children?"

And couldn't fight—at least not in this warm darkness, not when Kee Nang seemed the only solace for hard, cruel streets populated by teenage prostitutes lost to the night. So he believed in hell, after all, Chandler thought; he lived and worked in its heart.

"Because I can't think of anything better to do," he said harshly—then yielded to the touch of the woman, turned and added softly, "Because I don't like to see kids used, passed around, then thrown away."

"That happened to you, didn't it?" Kee Nang said quietly, her voice a caress.

Chandler, suddenly feeling very vulnerable and not caring, shrugged. "I guess my parents could have wanted me a little more. If they had, then maybe they would have stuck around a little longer."

"I think I can understand how you feel."

70

"I doubt it. From the look and sound of you, you come from what my ex-colleagues would call a 'good family.' I don't."

"It's true that I come from a 'good family.' But my father left us when I was very young. For a long time, it was very difficult for my mother and me."

Chandler placed his hand on top of the woman's, which still touched his arm. "Why did he leave?"

"He had a calling to the religious life. He had to follow his destiny."

Chandler smiled thinly, and resisted the impulse to shake his head in disgust; it was a story he was not unfamiliar with. "He got religion, so he ran out on you?"

"It's part of our culture to go if you are called. In fact, it was a great sacrifice for him; but each must give what he or she is asked to give."

"I don't think that's much of an excuse," Chandler said through tight lips.

Suddenly Kee Nang laughed lightly. "Chandler, he's *my* father! Why should *you* be so angry?"

Chandler rested his head on the steering wheel and took a deep breath, trying to erase the anger—and spite—from his heart. "You're right," he said quietly. "What your father did is none of my business." He paused, sighed, straightened up. "Wherever it is you live around here, why don't you invite the Chosen One up for a drink?"

The hand slipped away from his arm. "I'd rather not, Chandler. It's late, and I'm tired."

"Then let me take you to my place for a drink, Kee Nang. Just for a little while. Then I'll bring you back. If you don't drink booze, then you can have coffee, tea, juice, whatever."

71

I don't want you to leave because I'm lonely, Chandler wanted to say. But didn't.

"No, thank you," Kee Nang said, and got out of the car.

Chandler leaned across the seat and quickly rolled down the window on the passenger's side. "Kee Nang!"

The woman turned back, cocked her head slightly. "Yes, Chandler?"

"Maybe another time?"

"Maybe."

"Promise?"

"I never make promises, Chandler. I might not be able to keep them."

And then Kee Nang disappeared into the night.

Chapter Eight

"YOU MUST EAT, BOY," TIL SAID IN HIS LOW, RUMBLING voice as he set a bowl of bloodied oatmeal down in front of the cage imprisoning the Golden Child. "You have no choice; everybody has to eat."

The Golden Child remained silent, sat impassively in the center of the sinister cage staring straight ahead of him. Around the walls, the four perspiring, naked men continued their forced, mindless chanting.

After a few minutes, the giant shook his head in frustration, picked up the untouched bowl of tainted oatmeal and walked from the main storage room of the warehouse.

Only now did the boy move, reaching inside his robe to remove the twig with its three remaining leaves. He plucked another leaf, placed it in his mouth, then replaced the twig inside his robe.

Suddenly the voice of one of the naked chanters trailed off in a series of gurgling noises, and he pitched forward, collapsing from sheer exhaustion. The child quickly turned his head in that direction, and the expression of deep concern on his face changed to one of hope. He smiled, turned his body so that he was facing in the direction of the fallen chanter. He closed his eyes, and slowly, gradually, his body began once again to glow with shimmering golden light . . .

Chandler started, opened his eyes. He found himself sitting in the leather reclining chair in his study, in front of a snowy television set, where he had gone to fortify himself with a few shots of bourbon before listening to the calls that were recorded on his answering machine. He'd fortified himself right into unconsciousness, Chandler thought. With a grunt, he pushed himself out of his chair, turned on the light on his desk and shut off the television.

He didn't feel half bad, he thought as he regarded the answering machine with its glowing red indicator light. Not nearly as bad as he usually felt after a frustrating, dead-end day. In fact, he found he actually felt good, almost as if a fever had broken.

Chandler rubbed his eyes, pushed a button on the answering machine. The first call was from a father whose young daughter Chandler had found and brought safely home—almost a month before. He had received no payment, and the man was calling to say that he hadn't forgotten, that business had been slow, and that he'd be sending a payment as soon as he could.

"Right," Chandler said with a thin smile. "The check is in the mail."

The second voice, another man's, was sobbing. "Mr.

Jarrell," the breaking voice said, "I got your name and phone number from Lieutenant Boggs. Our little boy has been missing for two days. Tommy's a good little boy, Mr. Jarrell, and he's—"

Chandler abruptly pushed the *stop* button on the answering machine. Finding children, saving those he could, was the task to which he had decided to dedicate his life—but he was not ready to handle the rest of that particular call right now, in the middle of the night. For a little while, at least, he would try to relax. There would be more than enough to do tomorrow.

It slowly occurred to Chandler that something in the room was not right; it had changed. Or was changing. He turned to his right, was startled to see that the screen of his television set was glowing with a strange, fluorescent light: like a beam of sunlight viewed through a prism, it was refracting—virtually in slow motion—into a rainbow that was arcing over his head, across the room. The rainbow was growing . . .

Chandler stepped quickly to the television set and slapped his hand hard against the *On-Off* button; the set was already off. The rainbow continued to grow in size and intensity, and now that he was standing at the door to his study he realized that the rainbow was not coming from the set, but was reflecting from some source of light coming from outside his kitchen window.

Fire trucks or police cars on the street below, he thought. But he had not been awakened by sirens, and even now there was only the stillness of the night . . .

He slowly walked out of his study and into the kitchen, to the window—and had to put his hand to his mouth to stifle a startled shout.

Outside his window, in front of the stand of eucalyptus trees, a young boy effortlessly floated ten feet off the ground. The rainbow light which had penetrated his home was radiating from the golden glow surrounding the child . . .

Smiling and looking directly at him, the apparition slowly held out his hand, opened it. A bird with brilliant plumage soared from the child's hand and began to trill as, glowing in the night with rainbow colors of its own, it flew about among the eucalyptus trees, down the hillside, up again, heading directly toward where Chandler stood at the kitchen window . . .

The song of the bird was more beautiful than anything Chandler had ever heard; it seemed to fill his mind as well as fall on his ears, singing to his heart as well as his senses. And the bird was almost upon him now, turning night into multi-hued day, slowing as it prepared to land on his windowsill . . .

Chandler spun around and staggered away from the window. He tripped over a chair, fell painfully on his side. He was afraid he was going to be sick, and once again he put a hand over his mouth. He closed his eyes against the rainbow glow and, gagging, groped his way out of the kitchen, down the short stretch of hallway to his study. With his eyes closed he could not see the otherworldly light, but there was no way he could shut out the insistent trill of the singing bird outside his window. The singing had turned slightly plaintive, as if the bird wanted him to open the window . . .

"Jesus H. Christ," Chandler mumbled to himself as he fought against the panic and hysteria threatening to engulf him. "I've got to stop living like this."

He could possibly die right now, Chandler thought;

he could have a heart attack. His heart was pounding like a jackhammer inside his chest, and sweat ran in thick, milky rivulets off his body as, squinting now against the rainbow shimmer that filled the study, he picked up the phone and started to dial Emergency.

Chandler abruptly stopped dialing, slowly replaced the receiver in its cradle. There were no mental health clinics open at this time of night, Chandler thought; at least none that he would want to go to. And there was no psychiatrist who would be willing to see him. The only thing he could do was to get into his car and drive to a hospital, check himself in as a psychotic patient. But he didn't dare drive in his present condition, and if he called the police to come and get him, he would more than likely be taken to . . . a place he wouldn't like, perhaps a place even worse than this.

He had a sudden, almost overwhelming urge to run—anywhere. But he knew that if he did start running through the streets, he might never stop of his own accord: he would *be* stopped, and then he would be placed in some mental ward for a very long time.

"Easy, babe," he murmured, taking deep breaths. "You've got to be dreaming now. Just take it easy. No more pizza with anchovies before bedtime. I swear. Just get through this thing."

Suddenly he desperately wanted this to be a dream, and knew with absolute certainty that it was not; he was awake, in his own study, in the middle of the night. And he was hallucinating. Sweat continued to pour off his body as he gripped the edge of his desk to support himself; his heart continued to palpitate dangerously.

Any moment now his heart would burst in his chest, Chandler thought. And then he would die. Thirty years old, and he was going to die of a heart attack brought on by phantoms flitting and floating through his deranged mind . . .

Then the rainbow light winked out. The singing stopped, and it was night again; the only light in the room came from the desk lamp he had turned on earlier.

"No more bourbon, either. Calm *down*, Jarrell. There's an explanation."

He knew he had to do something to fight the terror within him and slow the beating of his heart; he had to find a way not to die.

"Maybe it's not a good idea to give up bourbon just yet."

He grabbed the half-full bottle from the table beside his chair, started to pour some in his glass, ended by taking three quick swallows from the bottle. The bourbon hit his empty stomach like a liquid depth charge, exploding warmth and numbness through his body. He took another long swallow, and then another. Within five minutes his heart had stopped pounding, and his breathing was almost normal.

He considered going outside to inspect the eucalyptus grove and decided against it. He knew he would find nothing there, because there had been nothing there. Kee Nang would get a kick out of *this* story, he thought. But he wasn't about to tell her. It had all been in his mind. What he had to do was clear to him: he would stay right where he was, drinking, and wait until morning, when he could go to see a doctor. And if he was drunk, that was okay; sobriety wasn't a requirement for admission to a mental hospital.

The most important thing was to stay awake; he must

not dream again until he was somewhere safe, with people who could take care of him.

"Not *too* hard on the bourbon, Jarrell," Chandler mumbled, taking another swallow from the bottle. "Maybe the kid and his bird will leave me alone if I leave some of the bottle for them . . ."

Sardo Numspa stalked into the main room of the warehouse. He glanced over at the fallen chanter, then at the child, who appeared to be in a state of deep meditation. The boy came out of his trance, looked up through the bars of his cage at the man. As he did so, his golden glow faded back to a dull bronze.

"By the time he finds you, it will be too late," Numspa said, his thin lips drawing back from his teeth in a cruel smile.

The phone rang.

Chandler jerked awake, momentarily startled and confused. He had fallen asleep—or passed out—on his feet, leaning against the desk. The bottle had slipped from his fingers, spilling its remaining contents out over a scatter rug. The study smelled of bourbon, and Chandler found that he had a splitting headache. Light was coming in through the windows—but, mercifully, it was the light of day.

The phone kept ringing, and Chandler stared at it. He could see no point in answering it, and he idly wondered if he would be allowed to use a phone in the booby hatch where he was bound to end up.

The phone continued to ring; finally, Chandler answered it.

"Yeah."

"Are you the guy looking for Cheryl Mosely?" It was a girl's voice.

Chandler screwed his eyes shut, took a deep breath, slowly exhaled. "Yeah."

"I know who she was with last Thursday."

"Who?"

The voice hesitated just a moment. "The poster says there's a reward."

"Yeah."

"Well, could you please meet me at the Church of Our Heavenly Savior in an hour or so? It's at the corner of Melrose and Lincoln. Just come to the back door and knock. I'll be waiting."

"I'll be there," Chandler said, then hung up and headed for the shower.

There just might be something more useful for him to do this morning than check into a mental hospital, he thought. There would always be time for that later.

Chapter Nine

CHANDLER—SHOWERED, SHAVEN AND DRESSED IN CLEAN clothes—winced as the bright morning sunlight knifed into his sore, bloodshot eyes. He slipped on a pair of sunglasses, walked down the hillside to where he had parked his car, and cursed when he saw that he had a flat tire. Mumbling obscenities under his breath, he moved around to the back, opened the trunk. He was just lifting out the jack when the new, blue Buick pulled up alongside him and stopped.

"What the hell are you doing here?" Chandler snapped as Kee Nang rolled down the window and smiled at him.

"Good morning, Chandler," Kee Nang said evenly.

"You're still keeping tabs on me."

"Am I?"

"Or are you on protection patrol?"

"At the moment, it seems that I'm going to give you a ride. You seem to be in a hurry to get somewhere."

The Church of Our Heavenly Savior turned out to be a crumbling frame house in a rundown neighborhood. Following Chandler's directions, Kee Nang pulled in the back, where a small parking lot had been cleared amid the rubble of a neighboring house which had recently been torn down.

"You wait here," Chandler said as he opened the door and got out of the car.

"But if this girl knows somebody who may have killed Cheryl Mosely, it's possible she also knows—"

"I haven't forgotten your kid. But you stay here. In Los Angeles, you never know what you're going to find behind closed doors."

Chandler walked up to the back door, pushed aside a broken neon sign that was hanging from its wires, and knocked lightly. A voice, which he recognized as belonging to the girl who had called him, whispered tentatively from the other side of the door.

"Rob? That you?"

"It's Chandler Jarrell. You phoned me a little while ago about Cheryl Mosely."

The door opened, and a girl Chandler estimated to be seventeen or eighteen slipped furtively out, quickly closing the door behind her. She was attractive, Chandler thought—at least as much of her as he could see. Her head was wrapped in a huge, red turban that came down almost to her eyebrows, and she wore a shapeless, flowing robe of the same color.

"I'm the one," the girl said, looking quickly around her.

"What can you tell me about Cheryl Mosely?"

"What about the reward?"

"I don't handle rewards, miss. That's up to the father—and he's not likely to give you any money if what you say doesn't lead to anything."

"Shit," the girl said, looking thoroughly crestfallen. "My old boyfriend's coming around to pick me up from this rathole. I told him I had gas money."

"So you don't know anything about Cheryl Mosely?"

"Yes. I know who she was with last Thursday. It's just that I was counting on the money . . ."

"How much gas money did you tell your boyfriend you had?"

The girl studied Chandler with her green eyes, blinked long lashes. "I think I mentioned fifty dollars."

"What's he picking you up in, a 747? How about twenty?"

The girl thought about it, shrugged. "Okay."

Chandler took two ten-dollar bills from his wallet, handed them to the girl. "So? Who was Cheryl Mosely with last Thursday?"

"Well, actually I know *where* she was—or at least I think I do. I know she had an appointment to get herself tattooed at Fettered Leather."

Chandler frowned. "Fettered Leather isn't a tattoo parlor."

"There's a guy who works out of a back room. He just does specialty work for regular customers, and friends of regular customers."

Chandler thought about it, nodded. "All right, you're earning your money. What else do you know?"

"Nothing. As a matter of fact, I barely knew her—we met in a place on the Strip. She just wanted someone to go with her when she got the tattoo." The girl paused, shook her head slightly, and her lips pulled back in a bittersweet, bemused smile. "Can you believe it? This Mosely kid goes off to get tattooed, and I join the Church of Our Heavenly Savior—who turns out to be a little fat guy who's been hitting on me all week."

"Did she tell you why she was getting the tattoo?"

"Sure. The Yellow Dragons make all their old ladies get a tattoo of the club insignia."

"What the hell are the Yellow Dragons?"

"Motorcycle gang—and *very* bad news guys."

"Do they have a meeting place? Some kind of clubhouse?"

"Beats me. I don't know about any clubhouse, but I know they hang out together at Pandora's Box—a real dump over in West Hollywood. That's where Cheryl met them. Like I say, mister, they're real bad news guys. If you want the same free advice I gave her, you won't mess with them."

The girl paused, looked over to her left when a battered Chevrolet convertible pulled into the rubble-strewn parking lot. The girl giggled, ripped off her turban. "How do I look?" she asked, rubbing a hand over her shaved head.

"Just great," Chandler replied in a flat voice as he turned and watched the girl run to the Chevrolet and get in. He turned back and was startled to find Kee Nang standing beside him; he had not heard the car door open or close, had not heard footsteps on the coarse gravel.

"When people believe in nothing," Kee Nang said quietly as she gazed at the cloud of dust left behind by the departing car, "they are ready to believe in anything."

"You should talk," Chandler said curtly as he wheeled and started back toward the Buick. He was upset by the ease with which the woman had been able to sneak up on him, and he wondered how long she had been standing there.

Chapter Ten

PANDORA'S BOX TURNED OUT TO BE A THOROUGHLY SEEDY looking bar advertising topless and bottomless dancing, with amateur shows every Wednesday night. Like something too mean to die, it stood by itself, a malignant hulk of stained and rotting wood, in a burned-out section of West Hollywood, next to the rotting hulk of what had once been a restaurant advertising, "No Topless, No Bottomless, No Video, Just Good Food."

When Chandler had driven up and parked across the street at midnight, there had been three big Harley-Davidsons outside the bar. It was now past three, and there were more than a dozen, including the one which had just been parked by a massive, barrel-chested man dressed in a yellow-stained leather jacket and pants. On the back of the jacket, outlined in black, was an insignia identical to the yellow dragon Chandler had seen on Cheryl Mosely's shoulder.

He looked across the seat at Kee Nang, who appeared to be sleeping. She was so beautiful, Chandler thought, and he smiled as he reached out and tenderly brushed a strand of black hair back from her high forehead.

"What do we do now?" Kee Nang asked in a clear voice as she opened one eye.

"We wait," Chandler replied curtly, embarrassed at being caught at such an unguarded—and revealing—moment. "When they split up, we'll single one out and politely ask him about Cheryl."

"And if he won't tell us?"

"We act real offended and ask him again—not so politely. But I can tell you right now that these guys don't have your kid."

"It is all part of your destiny. You will find the Golden Child."

"Listen," Chandler said carefully, losing a little patience, "even if your kid has been snatched, I don't buy he's some magical kid sent to bring good into the world."

"It is not important that you believe in the child. It is only important that you believe such good can exist in the world."

Chandler snorted. "Look around you, lady. You see any good in the world?"

Now Kee Nang sat up very straight, turned so that she was directly facing him. "Yes," she said firmly.

Embarrassed anew when he realized that she meant him, Chandler looked away. "You're a real piece of work, you know that? Get some sleep. I've got a feeling these guys stay up late." Almost unconsciously, he reached beneath the dashboard and touched the unlicensed Smith & Wesson taped there—just to make certain it was close at hand.

It was almost five-thirty in the morning before the bikers came out—and they exited *en masse,* which disturbed Chandler. He had hoped to single out one—hopefully thoroughly drunk—Yellow Dragon, put the gun to his head and question him about Cheryl Mosely. Now he could not do that—unless one stopped by the roadside to urinate, or otherwise became separated from the others.

Now there was absolutely no doubt that he was crazy, Chandler thought with a grim smile as he nudged Kee Nang awake and started up the car. He put it in gear and started off after the tight phalanx of motorcyclists who roared off in unison from the parking area in front of Pandora's Box. If he weren't crazy, he would be resting comfortably in a nice mental hospital right now, getting treatment from people who would most definitely agree that he was crazy if they could see what he was doing at the moment.

On his way to a psychiatrist or clinic he could have stopped downtown to see Ashley Boggs, told the police lieutenant what the girl had told him. That would have been the smart move . . .

Boggs would have listened patiently before telling him he'd blown twenty bucks. Boggs would have told him that Yellow Dragons drive motorcycles, not white vans, and they don't sit around all night singing, or humming, or chanting, or whatever the people in the house where Cheryl Mosely had been killed had been doing. Boggs would certainly have questioned a few of the Yellow Dragons . . . and would have learned nothing.

Still, right now he only had one lead to follow. And besides, he preferred real, if potentially lethal, Yellow Dragons to the rodent-faced one with fiery eyes he had seen in Hong's herb shop, and which occasionally flapped through his dreams.

He also had unfinished business to take care of. He had accepted three hundred and twenty-six dollars from a woman who probably couldn't afford it, and all she wanted was for her daughter's killer to be brought to justice.

Unwilling to risk detection by following directly behind the Yellow Dragons, he tracked the motorcycle convoy through the city by driving on parallel routes, monitoring their progress by listening for the roar of their bikes and catching an occasional sighting down a cross street. After a few minutes the convoy drove up a ramp of the Golden State Freeway, heading north. Knowing they would keep to a steady fifty-five miles per hour to avoid harassment from the state police, and not wanting to position himself too close behind them on the freeway, Chandler took his time driving around the block before cutting back and driving up the ramp to the freeway. He caught sight of them in the distance before settling in behind a tractor-trailer.

Forty-five minutes later he followed them off the exit at Palmdale, and once again tracked them by driving on parallel routes. When they suddenly disappeared from sight and their engines could no longer be heard, Chandler doubled back and drove slowly through the neighborhood until he found the bikes parked in a vacant lot next to what he assumed must be a house—it was surrounded by an eight-foot-high corrugated steel fence.

Chandler stopped the car, turned off the engine, then rested his head on the steering wheel and took a series of deep breaths in an effort to slow his pounding heart. This was definitely beginning to look like a bad idea, Chandler thought. But then, he had already been up all night, and had come this far . . .

And tearing open a young girl's throat in order to drain her body of blood was also a bad idea.

Also, he had come to believe that Kee Nang and her people—whatever their fantasies, and his—really were missing a child. The Yellow Dragons would certainly have no use for a five-year-old boy, but there could be some kind of link.

The people who killed Cheryl Mosely have the child. His destiny.

No time like the present to pursue his destiny.

Suddenly he sensed a strange presence, thought he heard the faint trill of a bird—although he was not certain whether it was real or only in his mind. He looked up—and started when he saw the bird with the brilliant plumage, the same one he had seen in the hallucination in his back yard, sitting on a wire above the car. Chandler quickly looked away; when he looked back, the bird was gone.

"What is it?" Kee Nang asked.

"Nothing," Chandler replied tersely. A goddam hallucination.

"What happened to your plan to single one out?"

"I made a mistake, okay?"

"Okay," Kee Nang said quietly.

"Don't worry. I came prepared for other eventualities. You wait here. If *anything* gives you the impression that something's happened to me, don't stick around. Go for help—fast."

Chandler reached under the dashboard for the Smith & Wesson. He checked the magazine to make sure it was full, then stuck the gun in his belt and got out of the car. Trying to appear casual in case anyone was watching, he angled across the street to the steel barrier. He tried the door cut into the fence, found it latched from the inside. He went around the corner into the lot, dragged one of the motorcycles over to the fence. He got up on the seat and peered over the fence. He saw the rear of a gray, ramshackle house. There was no one in sight at any of the windows; he sprang off the seat of the Harley, straddled the fence, then dropped down on the other side. He landed at a bad angle, crumpled in a heap. He cursed silently, rubbing his twisted ankle, then got up and hobbled as fast as he could across the junk-filled back yard to the rear door. He tested his ankle by putting his full weight on it, found that it was all right. Keeping flat against the wall, he leaned to one side and looked in the window of the door.

Three Yellow Dragons were sitting around a kitchen table, glasses of beer in their hands and feet propped up on a filthy oilskin tablecloth, talking.

Chandler took a deep breath, then tried the knob; it turned. He took another deep breath, turned the knob and shoved the door open. He quickly stepped into the room, braced with his feet apart, and used both hands to aim his pistol at a point midway between the three startled Yellow Dragons.

"Just sit tight," he said in a low voice, through clenched teeth. "Don't shout, and don't take your feet down off the table. Keep your hands where I can see them. Keep it low, because we don't want to wake anyone up. Remember: if I'm crazy enough to break in here like this, I'm certainly crazy enough to shoot all three of you without a second thought. I just want to ask you a few questions. You answer them to my satisfaction, and I'm long gone. Don't answer my questions, or try to get smart, and I'm going to put a bullet in each one of you real fast and I'm *still* going to be long gone. Got it?"

The three Yellow Dragons, drunk and bleary-eyed, exchanged quizzical looks; then the biggest of them, a man with long, gray hair that hung in greasy ringlets about his shoulders, looked at Chandler and lazily blinked.

"Are you kidding me, fool?"

"Cheryl Mosely. What did you do with her?"

"Who the fuck are you, asshole?" a second man with an acne-scarred face said as he set down his glass of beer and stood up—only to quickly sit down again when Chandler swung the Smith & Wesson around and pointed it at his head.

"I want to know what you did with Cheryl Mosely. And why."

Once again the men looked at one another, and then all three burst out laughing.

They weren't exactly being cooperative, Chandler thought; which meant that he was going to back away and try another day, another plan. There were just too many Yellow Dragons. He wouldn't necessarily be averse to firing shots over the heads of these three, or even nicking one—but then the nine or more other men in the house would be coming to see what happened, and he didn't have enough bullets in the gun.

"You're dead meat," the biggest of the men said casually. "Dead fucking meat."

Coming into Fort Apache had most definitely been a bad idea, Chandler thought as he took a step backward —the result of a hangover from too much bourbon, too many bad dreams, too much desperation.

He was almost out the door when something very hard hit him on the back of the head. He would have pulled the trigger on the gun if he could, but suddenly there was no feeling in his arms or legs.

"Shit," he said, or thought he said, as his knees collapsed under him and he fell face down on the floor.

Chapter Eleven

THE CHOSEN ONE WAS SUFFERING TERRIBLY, KEE NANG thought as she stared at the spot where Chandler had disappeared over the fence. Some of his distress she understood perfectly well. So much had changed in this song, this world, in the thousand years since the last Golden Child had come. Science had radically altered the song, and few educated men or women of the West any longer took seriously the idea that bringers of wondrous good—like the *Gompen Tarma*—could exist, along with beings who would surface from their own, sour song to try to stop the mission of the Golden Child.

Not for nothing, she thought grimly, had this song plunged into what was called the Dark Ages after the death of the last Golden Child. This time the future could be even worse if Chandler Jarrell could not save the current *Gompen Tarma:* there would be pestilence, death and destruction around this world for a thousand years. All progress would stop, and many millions would die of starvation as technology ground to a halt.

Only the Chosen One could prevent it, and she could not understand why Chandler Jarrell, a man of the West with deep personal wounds, should have been chosen by That Sings. But then, she knew that such matters were always beyond the ken of beings in any song—*Gompen Tarmas,* humans, or creatures from the low songs. There were Golden Children, and there were Chosen Ones to protect them; there was no *reason* for such things.

Still, Kee Nang thought, her own task would have been made so much easier—or even unnecessary—if the Chosen One had come from an Oriental culture. Then her mission, experience and knowledge would not have to be constantly explained, and met by a wall of disbelief and mockery. And the Chosen One would not have to suffer so. She had understood the risk she would be taking with Chandler's Western-oriented mind when she had first begun to explain his mission, and hers, and tried to get him to take her seriously—if not out of curiosity, then out of fear. Now, perhaps, he was beginning to take her seriously, but he was in constant danger of splitting apart because of things that were happening to him which he could not reconcile with his view and understanding of reality.

She had been particularly distressed by Chandler's reaction to the portrait of Sardo Numspa in Dr. Hong's shop. That reaction had led her to believe that Chandler had seen Sardo Numspa before, in dreams; if that were the case, it could mean that the deadliest creature from the lowest, sourest song had ascended through the dimensional layers to attack the child. If Sardo Numspa was loose in this song, Kee Nang knew that the peril to the Golden Child, the Chosen One, and the world was greater than it had ever been; for the first time, the goodness and beauty in this song was in danger of being sucked away—forever.

A Chosen One who did not even believe in songs different from his own against Sardo Numspa, with the soul of this world at stake, seemed a mismatch almost too great to comprehend, Kee Nang thought. Yet—the incomprehensible power that was That Sings had chosen Chandler Jarrell . . .

Truly, she thought with a grim smile and a slight shake of her head, That Sings was inscrutable.

But now she had other things in this dimensional plane to worry about, Kee Nang thought as she got out of the car. She had no idea what Chandler intended to do inside the motorcyclists' clubhouse, but it was an incontestable fact that he was one man against a dozen or more. It was up to her to protect the Chosen One; that was her job, her destiny, and she recognized it as being as important as the one Chandler refused to acknowledge. If the Chosen One were killed, then the Golden Child would perish, along with the world.

She could not stop the Chosen One from doing whatever it was he'd decided to do, nor did she wish to; something the Yellow Dragons knew could very well be the key to where the Golden Child was being held. All she could do was try to make certain Chandler was kept from harm as he pursued his destiny . . .

Kee Nang went out into the middle of the street. She drew in a deep breath in order to focus her *chi*, then sprinted forward. When she was four feet from the fence she leaped into the air, caught the top of the fence with her hands and used the momentum of her powerful leap to carry her over the top. She landed lightly on the balls of her feet on the other side, rolled to absorb the force of the shock, came up running low across the dirt and garbage that was the front yard to the side of the house, where she pressed flat against a wall, watching and listening. There were no sounds of alarm from inside the house, and Kee Nang assumed that she had not been seen. Surprise was not absolutely essential, but it was desirable; the twelve or more murderous thugs inside the house could stretch her talents and capabilities to their limit.

She inched along the side of the house, peered through a dirt-smeared window into an empty living room. Perhaps, she thought, all of the Yellow Dragons were dead drunk and asleep. Perhaps no one had heard Chandler enter, and the Chosen One had found one man alone, and was not in danger.

Perhaps not. She had to go in.

She tried the window and then the front door, found them locked. Once again she leaped into the air, caught hold of an eave, and effortlessly swung up to a balcony extending from a room on the second floor. She peered in a window, saw no one in the gloom inside. The window was open; moving silent as a shadow, Kee Nang opened it and slipped into the house. She was halfway across the room before she saw the dark shapes of eight men in sleeping bags around the walls of the room. Now one of the men stirred, opened his eyes, and blinked in disbelief when he saw Kee Nang.

"Holy shit," the man said, sitting up in his sleeping bag and nudging the man in the bag next to him. "Hey, Mike, look at what we've got here. Who says there's no Santa Claus?"

Santa Claus would have to bring this particular Yellow Dragon new front teeth at the least, Kee Nang thought as she leaped across the room and launched herself into the air, spinning to gain momentum, then lashing out with her right heel to catch the man in the mouth, knocking away teeth and consciousness. As she landed she spun again, caught the second man in the jaw with her elbow; he slumped over, was still. Two other men, slack-jawed and disoriented, struggled to get out of their bags. In an instant, Kee Nang was back across the room—spinning, kicking, punching. When she had knocked those two unconscious, she slowly backed into the center of the room, went into a crouch and slowly turned as she moved her arms in front of her body in an intricate *kata*, waiting for any of the others to attack.

But the other men remained asleep; one in a corner started to snore loudly; another grunted, rolled over . . .

Kee Nang darted out of the room and down a dark, narrow hallway to a flight of stairs. She silently descended to the first floor, paused when she heard voices off to her right.

"I don't have to cut him up to get rid of him. I stuff him in a garbage bag and dump him off-road in Los Padres."

"What if some animal drags him out into a campsite?"

"So what? He gonna spoil some little old lady's dinner?"

Keeping her back to the wall, she slipped down the corridor, stopped outside a half-open door, peered through the crack between the jamb and the door into the kitchen.

Chandler, the hair on the back of his head matted with blood, was slumped in a chair a few feet away from where Kee Nang was standing. His hands were tied behind his back, which was to Kee Nang. Facing him in a semicircle were four Yellow Dragons, the expressions on their faces a mixture of bemusement and cruelty. Chandler moaned, shook his head.

"You've got to be the stupidest motherfucker on the face of the earth," one of the men said as he removed a heavy, metal-studded leather belt from the loops of his jeans. "What the fuck did you think you were doing, coming in here?"

"Actually," Chandler croaked hoarsely, "I've been thinking of buying a new bike, and I wanted to get your opinion on the new Harleys."

Kee Nang grimaced and raised her eyebrows, then winced as the man who had spoken snapped the tip of the belt against Chandler's left arm.

"How does that feel, asshole?" the scar-faced man with the belt said. "Smarts, huh? That was just your arm. Wait until you feel the end of this belt in your balls and on your face."

"Did you people kill Cheryl Mosely?"

The belt snapped out, struck Chandler's other arm, ripping his shirt. Blood began to flow, soaking into the torn fabric.

Kee Nang abruptly pushed the door open and stepped into the room. In the two or three seconds the startled Yellow Dragons spent staring at her in astonishment, Kee Nang's powerful fingers had untied the knots in the rope binding Chandler to the chair. She tossed the rope to one side, pulled him to his feet by the back of his shirt.

"I think it's time to leave, Chandler," she said as she

went down into a crouch and began weaving her hands in front of her in a *kata* as she planned her attack. She would take out the biggest man first, she thought, perhaps with a spinning high kick to the face. At the same time, she would slash with the sides of her hands at the windpipes of the two men flanking him. She would worry about the fourth man when she saw their relative positions after the initial attack . . .

To Kee Nang's amazement, Chandler suddenly stepped in front of her and raised his arms. "I'm all right, Kee Nang," he said in a low voice over his shoulder. "Stay behind me. I'll get us to the door; whatever happens, you make sure you get away—and keep going."

"Ah," was all Kee Nang said as she came out of her crouch and stepped backward.

The man farthest to the right, the biggest, was the first to recover from his shock. With a roar, he charged Chandler, and Kee Nang was impressed with Chandler's speed and power as he sidestepped the rush, then grabbed a handful of the man's long, gray hair and used the man's own weight and momentum to fling him across the room. The man crashed into a sideboard, slumped slowly to the floor.

"These guys are real sensitive types," Chandler said to Kee Nang over his shoulder. "They just act tough."

"You should talk."

The belt snapped out, but Chandler ducked under it. The scar-faced man leaped forward and threw a punch that missed Chandler's head but struck his bleeding shoulder. Chandler grunted with pain, but came back with a right cross that caught the man squarely on the jaw, knocking him cold.

While the two men left on their feet began to circle

Chandler warily, Kee Nang saw that the gray-haired man Chandler had flung across the room was struggling to get up. He opened a drawer, took out a butcher knife . . .

Kee Nang, sensitive to—and touched by—Chandler's determination to protect her, glanced around to make certain the Chosen One's back was to her; then, in two quick bounds, she was across the room, bringing her foot up hard into the gray-haired man's groin. The Yellow Dragon groaned, bent over to clutch at his groin, went down on his knees. Instantly, Kee Nang returned to her position behind Chandler's back.

"You all right?" Chandler snapped, turning his head slightly.

"Yes," Kee Nang said, patting him on the back. "You're doing wonderfully."

"Don't worry."

"I'm not."

Chandler brought a chair crashing down over the head of one of his two remaining opponents—as yet another, sleepy-eyed, Yellow Dragon stumbled into the kitchen.

The new arrival entered the room just in time to see Kee Nang's form flying through the air at his head. Kee Nang brought her heel crashing into his temple, and the man slammed back into the doorjamb, slumped to the floor, unconscious. Kee Nang landed lightly on her feet, then backed up against a wall and waited, ready to go to Chandler's aid if he needed it. He didn't. He ducked under a wild, roundhouse swing, caught his opponent with a sharp uppercut that lifted the man off his feet and sent him tumbling out through the open back door to land unconscious in a pile of garbage.

Panting, Chandler staggered backward until he came

up against a countertop next to a sink. Smiling, Kee Nang went over to him. She turned on the water in the sink, wetted a washcloth and gently pressed it against the back of his head.

"You all right?" Chandler gasped.

"Yes, thanks to you. You are a very brave man—as, naturally, the Chosen One would be. Your head . . .?"

"It's all right," Chandler replied, looking around the room. He frowned when he saw the fifth man slumped unconscious in the doorway. "Where the hell did he come from?"

"He came in a couple of minutes ago," Kee Nang said easily. "He must have been very drunk, because he tripped over his own feet, fell down and just stayed there. He must have hit his head on the doorjamb."

Chandler studied Kee Nang. "Where the hell did *you* come from?"

Kee Nang shrugged, grinned. "You know I've been following you. It's my job to protect you."

"Yeah," Chandler grunted, and took the washcloth away from his head.

"Are you all right, Chandler?"

"I had a bad hangover when I came in here, but these guys cured it." He paused to fully catch his breath. When he spoke again, there was real anger in his voice. "As for you, don't you ever do anything as stupid as this again, Kee Nang. Thank you for helping me. You probably saved my life, but you could have been killed. I told you to wait in the car. Promise me you won't ever pull a stunt like this again, no matter what's happening to me."

"I promise I shall always feel safe when I'm with you," Kee Nang replied meekly.

"Kee Nang—!"

"You're some fighter."

Chandler snorted with disgust, then began searching around the kitchen until he found the Smith & Wesson under the lip of a counter, where it had slid when he had been sapped. He picked up the gun, glanced warily at the ceiling.

"If the others slept through this," Kee Nang said, "I think they'll sleep through anything. I don't think you have to worry about them, but I'll stand here by the door and listen. Why don't you ask the one on his knees over there the questions you came to ask?"

Chandler put the gun back in his waistband, then walked over to the gray-haired man, who was still clutching his groin as he rocked back and forth, moaning. Chandler pulled the big man to his feet by the hair, then threw him against the sink. He turned on the water, pushed the man's head under it, face up.

"You had a girl tattooed with a dragon!" Chandler snapped, holding the struggling man's head under the water. "What happened to her?!"

The man spluttered, and Chandler took his head from under the running water. The Yellow Dragon coughed and stared at Chandler with glassy eyes, which slowly came into focus—and glinted with fear. "Huh?"

Chandler slammed his fist into the man's stomach. The Yellow Dragon clutched at his belly and doubled over, then slumped to his knees once again.

"The girl!" Chandler said as he yanked the man's head back by the hair. "What happened to her?!"

"What girl?" the man said in an agonized whisper. "I don't know what you're talking about, assh—man."

"She was just a kid—blond, very fair skin, freckles, green eyes. You made her have a yellow dragon tattooed on her left shoulder."

104

The man thought hard about it, finally nodded. "Oh, *that* girl."

"Did you kill her?"

"Are you kidding me, man?"

"What happened to her?!"

"We sold her, man."

Chandler hesitated, shook his head in bewilderment. "You say you *sold* her?"

"Yeah, man," the Yellow Dragon said, glancing back and forth between Chandler and Kee Nang, obviously not understanding why Chandler should be so upset. "We sold her to a guy by the name of Tommy Tong, a weirdo who runs a bar on Broadway. He said he needed a girl because he'd sold his soul to the devil and he needed her blood. It sounded like pretty heavy duty shit Tommy was into, but we were short of cash."

Kee Nang felt the muscles in her stomach tighten, and she watched as Chandler quickly glanced up at her. Now, perhaps, the Chosen One would start to listen, she thought. Perhaps.

"You *sold* her?!" Chandler said to the kneeling Yellow Dragon, grimacing in disgust.

"Yeah, man," the Yellow Dragon mumbled as he struggled to get to his feet. "I just told you that. I don't see what the prob—"

"Shut up!" Chandler shouted, and hit the man square in the face with his fist. Spraying blood from his broken nose, the man toppled backward to the floor and lay still.

Chandler looked at Kee Nang, tears in his eyes and pain in his voice. "They sold her," he said in quiet disbelief, then turned and walked unsteadily out the back door, stepping over the unconscious man lying in the pile of garbage.

Kee Nang followed Chandler out of the house, across the back lawn and through the gate to his car.

Chandler released a long, pent-up sigh, reached out and gently gripped Kee Nang's arms. "Thanks again, lady. If not for you, I'd probably look like cat food now. You saved my ass."

"Ah, but then you saved me, too. Let's say we saved each other."

"I don't want you with me any more, Kee Nang," Chandler said in a low voice, staring hard into her eyes. "And I don't want you following me."

"If you don't want me following you, then you must let me come with you."

"This business is starting to get very heavy and dangerous. I don't want you to get hurt. Today you were lucky; next time you might not be so lucky."

"I could say the same words to you."

"This is my work, Kee Nang, and a certain amount of risk goes with the territory. If you think I've forgotten your boy, I haven't; and I won't. He's five years old, you say. Oriental, I assume?"

"Yes, Chandler," Kee Nang said softly. "He's five years old, and he's Oriental."

"I'll be looking for him. Since you won't tell me where you live or how to get in touch with you, I'll leave word with your friend who owns the herb shop if I find out anything."

"I will stay with you, Chandler."

"Damn it, Kee Nang! Don't be stubborn. Something terrible is happening to—something terrible is happening."

Kee Nang studied Chandler's face, felt tears welling in her eyes. She could feel his torment radiating from him like fever heat. But she dared not tell him the

106

whole truth; she knew he would not accept it, and she believed it would only cause him further torment. She would risk pushing him away from her—and the *Gompen Tarma*—forever.

The Chosen One had to find his own way, she thought.

"Are you beginning to believe me, Chandler?" she asked in the same, small voice.

"I'll tell you what I believe. I believe somebody's taken a child. You say the child isn't yours. Since I can't think of any reason why a mother would deny that a kidnapped child was hers, I think that's the truth. If the boy isn't yours, then he belongs to another member of whatever religious cult you belong to. For some reason, you won't tell me about the group, or anything else that might help me." Chandler paused, raised his eyebrows inquiringly. "Will you?"

"Everything I've told you is the truth, Chandler. There is no 'religious cult' to talk about."

Chandler sighed, shook his head. When he spoke now, there was a hard edge of anger and frustration in his tone. "Was the boy taken by enemies of your movement? Is this some kind of revenge or blackmail scheme? What is it they want you to give them before they return the child? For the boy's sake, why don't you just tell me who took him?"

"I've told you we don't know who took him, Chandler," Kee Nang said, and she suddenly felt short of breath. Very softly, in a voice just above a whisper, she added: "I think you do."

"*I* do?" Anger—and not a little fear—swam in Chandler's dark, expressive eyes.

"I think so," Kee Nang said carefully, aware that she was now treading on very dangerous ground, gambling

107

with the Chosen One's sanity. "I believe it possible that you have been given more than any Chosen One before you, perhaps because the age we live in now is so very different from any other age in which a Golden Child was born. You have been given the most, because you have a greater burden than any Chosen One before you."

"Have it your way, lady!" Chandler snapped as he jerked the car door on Kee Nang's side open. "I told you I'll be looking—hard—for your missing boy, because I believe that much. But if that little kid is damaged in any way because you wouldn't stop playing games with me and save me some time, I'm going to be coming after you people with more than a butterfly net. I'll be doing some serious investigating of your outfit, if only so I can punch out your leader. Think about it, Kee Nang! I really hope I'm reaching you!"

It is not me you must reach, Kee Nang thought as she slid into the seat. She made no move to wipe away the tears that flooded her eyes. *You must somehow reach yourself, and the world will perish if you fail.*

Chapter Twelve

CHANDLER SAT IN THE STATION WAGON ACROSS THE street from Tommy Tong's Seafood House, watching. The bar and restaurant was in a fairly respectable part of town, yet he had seen very few customers—respectable or otherwise—pass through the puddle of garish neon light that spilled out into the night from the half-broken sign above the entrance.

There was an almost palpable aura of evil about this place, Chandler thought, and it involved more than the fact that the owner of the restaurant was almost certainly responsible for the murder of Cheryl Mosely. The restaurant was certainly nowhere near as tawdry or ominous as Pandora's Box and the Yellow Dragons' clubhouse had been, yet, looking at it, Chandler was filled with an immense sense of foreboding which he did not understand. He glanced at Kee Nang to see if she felt it too. She looked calm. The red light splashing on—polluting—the sidewalk in front of the restaurant made him somehow feel as if he was staring into the mouth of hell . . .

And he suddenly knew with absolute and chilling certainty that he would find something inside Tommy Tong's Seafood House which would mark him and change his life permanently.

Tommy said he sold his soul to the devil.

"This time wait," Chandler said in a low but commanding voice to the woman sitting next to him.

Kee Nang did not reply.

He took the Smith & Wesson from beneath the dashboard, stuck it in his belt next to his spine, beneath his tweed sports jacket, then got out of the car and walked across the street. Afraid that if he hesitated he might not go in at all, Chandler picked up his pace as he stepped up on the curb and strode into the restaurant.

The place was virtually empty, except for three patrons at the bar, two couples in the restaurant section, and some of the help eating supper at a table in the rear. He started back, but was intercepted by the burly bartender.

"What you want, pally?"

"How do you know 'pally' doesn't simply want to eat?"

"You no want to eat here, pally."

"As a matter of fact, you're right. I want to talk to Tommy Tong."

"He no here, pally."

Chandler glanced over the bartender's shoulder, saw a door marked *Manager* in an alcove behind the table where the help was eating; there was light coming from beneath the door.

"Yeah, well, I think I'll go see for myself," Chandler said, placing his hand on the bartender's chest and pushing him aside.

The man grabbed Chandler's wrist, started to pull him back and around. Chandler went with the pressure on his arm, then abruptly fired a right cross that connected with the man's chin. The bartender's head snapped back, his knees gave way, and he crumpled to the hardwood floor. Chandler wheeled around, fists clenched, ready to fight anyone else who tried to stop him. The patrons at the bar quickly turned away when Chandler glared at them, looked back down into their drinks; the help at the back table resumed eating; the two couples in the restaurant section appeared not to have even noticed. Chandler strode quickly down the length of the restaurant to the door in the alcove at the back. He tried the knob, found that it turned. He opened the door and stepped in.

He found himself in a spacious office very dimly lit by recessed fluorescent lamps, half of which were burned out, and redolent with a smell of burning incense which made Chandler slightly nauseous. The office was bare of decoration, except for a heavy, somber-hued tapestry which covered the entire rear wall. In front of the tapestry was a desk, and behind the desk sat a man whose head and shoulders were hidden in shadow. Only his hands, turning the pages of what appeared to be a ledger, were visible, fish-pale in a bright, tightly focused cone of light projected by a high-intensity lamp set on a corner of the desk.

Chandler closed the door behind him, pushed the

punch-button lock in the knob. Without stopping his work, the man at the desk began speaking in Chinese.

"This isn't the help, Tong," Chandler said in a low voice. "My name's Jarrell, and I've come to hear everything you know about a murdered girl by the name of Cheryl Mosely. I'm betting that you slit her throat, you blood-eating son-of-a-bitch."

The hands stopped turning the pages in the ledger, and the man leaned forward into the light . . .

The young, Oriental thug was wearing a rock band T-shirt beneath a leather flight jacket. Behind him, visible now that the glare from the high-intensity lamp was blunted, sword handles protruded from two zebraskin sheaths hanging from a loop sewn into the tapestry.

Suddenly Chandler felt his throat constrict, and his heart began to pound. The room began to spin, and he backed up until he came up against the wall.

This was not an opportune moment to pass out, he thought as he shook his head, trying to clear it; if he did, this man would most certainly kill him. He knew he had to act, get the gun out of his waistband, but he felt paralyzed . . .

"Who the fuck are you, man?" Tommy Tong asked in an almost casual tone.

Chandler reached up with a trembling hand, wiped a sheet of sweat from his forehead before it could run into his eyes. "Where's the kid?" he asked in a voice so hoarse and strained that he hardly recognized it as his own.

"What kid?" The man in the rock band T-shirt and leather flight jacket seemed more amused than angry.

"*You* killed Cheryl Mosely," Chandler said, suddenly experiencing absolute certainty about what he was saying. More words, giving voice to thoughts and fears he had tried to ignore and bury, came tumbling out of him. "You slit her throat, and your buddies have been trying to feed her blood to the little boy you stole from the monks in the temple in Tibet. Where are you keeping that kid, Tong? Tell me quick, or I'm going to blow your fucking head off."

He hadn't quite gotten it right, Chandler thought as he fumbled for his gun with hands and fingers that felt like gum rubber. It wasn't Tommy Tong's head that was going to be missing—and this occurred to him in the brief moment that it took the young Oriental to react to his words. Moving with incredible speed, Tommy Tong leaped from his chair, reached behind him and drew the two swords from their zebra-skin sheaths.

Chandler felt as if he was moving in slow motion; while he fumbled behind his back beneath the folds of his jacket for his gun, the Oriental lithely leaped up on top of the desk, hopped down, then advanced on Chandler, the saw-toothed swords in his hands weaving a criss-cross pattern in the air on a level with Chandler's head. Another three or four steps . . .

"*Hai!*" Kee Nang cried as she stepped through a fold in the tapestry.

The distraction was just enough to spoil Tommy Tong's concentration, and aim. Chandler ducked away as one sword whistled over his head and the second grazed his left shoulder, slashing open his jacket but not cutting flesh. He lost his balance, stumbled and fell back against the wall as the Oriental prepared to strike again.

"*Hai!*"

Chandler winced, dropped to the floor and instinctively covered his head with his hands, expecting at any

113

moment to feel the jagged teeth of the blades biting into, slicing through, him. When nothing happened, he looked up—to witness an eerie ballet of grace, speed, and death.

Kee Nang was standing in the middle of the room, crouched, with her hands and arms weaving an elaborate figure-eight pattern in front of her face. Tommy Tong raised the sword in his right hand, swung it at Kee Nang's head. Moving with blinding speed, she blocked the strike with a forearm, spun away from a strike with the second sword, came back in and fired a side kick into the man's ribs. Tommy Tong yelped in pain and surprise, backed up two steps, recovered and came back at Kee Nang with both swords whirling in front of his body like a two-piece buzzsaw. With no way to parry the two swords, Kee Nang executed a back flip that carried her higher and farther than anything Chandler had ever seen in Olympic gymnastics competition—or anywhere else. She landed lightly on the balls of her feet on top of Tommy Tong's desk. A sword flashed through the air at her knees; she hopped over the sword, simultaneously firing a flying front kick that grazed the man's shoulder, spun him around and backed him up.

Now, showing newfound respect for Kee Nang's skills and speed, Tommy Tong had decided to take his time. While Kee Nang remained perched on top of the desk, Tong crouched and advanced slowly, swinging the swords on a level with her knees.

As good as Kee Nang was, Chandler thought, she was no match, finally, for a man with two swords; first she was going to lose her legs, and then her life.

The realization that Kee Nang was going to die horribly unless he roused himself to some kind of action cleared Chandler's senses, galvanized his muscles. He snatched the gun from his waistband, aimed carefully. He could not fire directly at Tommy Tong without risk of missing and hitting Kee Nang, so he pumped a bullet into the desk lamp. As glass and sparks flew, the man wheeled around, stared wide-eyed at the gun in Chandler's hand.

"Freeze, motherfucker!" Chandler shouted, scrambling to his feet and aiming the gun with both hands at Tommy Tong's right kneecap. He did not want to kill the Oriental, for at the moment Tommy Tong was their only link to the site where the little Tibetan boy was being held—and starved.

The Chinese stared back at Chandler. Hatred smoldered in the man's black eyes as he slowly raised the blades over his head.

"Easy now, motherfucker," Chandler cautioned. "Drop the swords, or I'm going to put you in a wheelchair for the rest of your life." He paused, looked in wonder at Kee Nang. "All that stuff . . . how the hell do you do that?"

"Years of practice," Kee Nang replied with a faint smile.

"Yeah, yeah," Chandler said, shaking his head in disbelief. "But how do you do it?"

Both blades flashed in the dim light, came flying through the air . . .

Chandler dove to one side as the swords sailed over his head and embedded themselves in the wall behind him. He rolled on one shoulder, came up on one knee with his gun aimed at the place where Tommy Tong had been standing. He squeezed off two shots, the twin explosions of the gun reverberating loudly in the closed space—but the Oriental was no longer there. Chandler heard a door slam shut behind the tapestry, realized that Tommy Tong had left the same way Kee Nang had entered.

Chandler sprang to his feet, leaped over the desk and yanked the tapestry from the wall.

"Chandler—?!"

But Chandler was already out the back door, sprinting down a dark and narrow alleyway. Tommy Tong was nowhere to be seen . . .

"Chandler, duck!"

Kee Nang's voice seemed to come from right behind him, but there was no time to duck. Suddenly a body crashed into the backs of his knees, and he went down a fraction of a second before a sword flashed from the black mouth of an even narrower alley to his left and sang in the air over his head, ruffling his hair.

Chandler struggled to his knees, winged a shot into the blackness at the mouth of the alley—but there was no one there. Worried about Kee Nang, he quickly glanced behind him; Kee Nang was already on her feet, looking down at him.

"Could you please be more careful, Chandler?" Kee Nang said mildly.

"I thought I told you to wait in the car!"

Chandler scrambled to his feet and, with the gun held ready in front of him, darted into the narrower alley. After thirty yards he slowed when the alley suddenly broadened into a relatively large, moonlit circular area blocked off at the far end by a high fence. He emerged from the narrow corridor, then abruptly stopped. He gagged, and was almost sick.

Tommy Tong had obviously had it in mind to climb over the fence, and most of him had almost made it. His outstretched arms were still up, fingers tightly clasping the top of the fence, as if he were still getting ready to haul most of him up and over it. But that was as far as he was going to get without his head, which was ten feet away, skewered on the tip of yet another sword. Blood still spurted from the stump of his neck, and the expression on Tommy Tong's face in the bright moonlight was one of total astonishment.

Chandler, gun held out in front of him, slowly turned, looking for whoever it was who had killed the Oriental. But the circular area was bare, without even a garbage can for someone to hide behind. It was a barren *cul-de-sac*. Yet, he had not passed anyone on the way in, indeed couldn't have in the narrow passageway . . .

He had been only seconds behind Tong, and not even a giant kangaroo could have hopped over that fence before he'd arrived . . .

Giant kangaroo.

It was a damn good thing there was nobody here, Chandler thought as he felt hysterical laughter building in him, because his hands were shaking so badly that he couldn't hold the gun straight.

He continued to turn until he found himself pointing the gun at Kee Nang, who was standing just beyond the mouth of the alley. He lowered the gun, swallowed in an attempt to contain his sick laughter.

"Oh, my," Kee Nang said in a small voice as she stared at the decapitated corpse.

Chandler looked down at his hands, which continued to shake violently. He tried to slip the gun back into his waistband, and couldn't. He dropped it into his jacket pocket. "Oh, my," he said, and began to chuckle. The laughter would not stay bottled up any longer; his hysteria felt as if it was pressing against the back of his teeth, threatening to shatter and blow them from his mouth.

He staggered past Kee Nang, just managed to enter the mouth of the alley before he reeled, fell back against a dank, night-cold brick wall. He was hyperventilating, and white spots had begun to dance in front of his eyes.

He felt a hand touch his chest, begin to gently massage it. Gradually his vision began to clear, his heart stopped pounding so violently, and his breathing became more regular. He found himself staring into the face of Kee Nang.

"Talk to me, Chandler," Kee Nang said quietly. "It will help; it will make the terror go away."

Chandler rested his head against the brick wall, bit off a giggle. "Well, the good news is that I don't have to worry any more about losing my mind; my mind is long gone, mama. A giant kangaroo hopped away with it."

"It isn't true, Chandler. Keep talking."

Chandler glanced back toward the headless corpse hanging from the fence, resisted the impulse to giggle again. Or cry. "What would you say if I told you that I'd met that guy before—not somebody who looks like him, but *that guy*—in my dreams? I've seen that guy, and his swords."

"I would say that I know you have met him," Kee Nang replied matter-of-factly as she continued to massage his chest.

Chandler studied her face, blinked. "Huh? How do you know?"

Kee Nang hesitated just a moment, then made her decision. "I have sent you dreams, Chandler."

"You *what?!* What the hell are—?"

Kee Nang raised her other hand and gently but firmly

118

pressed it over his mouth. "Don't talk, Chandler; not now. Just listen—and consider the possibility that what I tell you is true, because it is. Remember that if it *is* true, then you are not mad, as you fear.

"There is a phenomenon known as 'dream transmission.' I can't explain how or why the phenomenon exists; only now, through the insights quantum mechanics is giving scientists into the nature of time, space and matter, are we all beginning to probe some of the deeper aspects of what we call 'reality.' Simply accept that I have sent you dreams. I know how much you have suffered because of them, but, because you are a Westerner, I did not know how else . . . I had, I felt, to somehow prepare the way. As it was, you dismissed me as insane when I first approached you and spoke of the *Gompen Tarma* and new forces loose in the world; now you are dismissing yourself as insane. You have *not* lost your mind, Chandler. Believe this; trust me. Your dreams have been messages."

Chandler reached up, firmly grasped Kee Nang's wrist and took her hand from his mouth. He nodded in the direction of Tommy Tong's corpse. "*You* knew that man? You told me—"

"*Now* I know who and what he was; he was one of the men who took the *Gompen Tarma*. I did not know that before. I had never seen him, or any of the other . . . men . . . responsible."

"But you just said you sent me the dreams—"

"I did not send you the dream or dreams in which you saw this man. It means you are receiving dream transmissions from . . . elsewhere."

"What the hell do you mean, 'elsewhere'?"

"Thank you for listening to me, Chandler," Kee Nang said, bowing her head slightly. "You have no idea how much the prospect of having this conversation frightened me."

"Hey, what have I got to lose? You can only get so crazy—I think."

Kee Nang took a deep breath, slowly exhaled. "I believe the Golden Child himself has been sending you dreams. I will have to check with Kala, but I'm certain there is no record of something like that happening in all of the thousands of years that Golden Children have been sent to humans. If it is true, Chandler, it is a wondrous thing."

Chandler thought about it for some time, frowned. "Some of the things I've dreamed I'm not sure even the kid would have seen, or know about," he said at last.

"Don't be certain of that. However, it is even possible That Sings has transmitted dreams to you and acted as your guide."

"What? Who sings?"

"*That* Sings. The universe."

"Are you talking about God?"

"I can't be sure what image is in your mind when you speak of 'God,' so I can't say. That Sings is . . ." Kee Nang shrugged. "That Sings is the song we all are here, all that everything is—in other places. The words, That Sings, are a translation from Tibetan—imprecise, but close. It is most difficult for me to understand how—or why—That Sings would transmit dreams to you, but it seems a definite possibility in this case. Again, I will have to ask Kala."

Chandler laughed. "Difficult for *you* to understand?! I love it!"

"It is not important that either of us understand—or even think about—these matters, Chandler. It is only important that you believe me when I tell you that what is happening is real. You are *not* going insane—but you do have the greatest burden any human has ever been asked to bear."

"Who killed that guy hanging from the fence? The goddam alley's empty, and I don't believe anybody could have climbed over that fence before I got here; I was just seconds behind him."

It was some time before Kee Nang spoke. "Tommy Tong was killed so that he could not be forced to tell you where the *Gompen Tarma* is being held."

"Yeah, but *who*—?"

"I believe he was killed by a creature similar to what you might call a . . . demon."

"Oh, shit," Chandler said, closing his eyes as he felt tears welling in them. The hysterical laughter stirring in his chest, momentarily held at bay by Kee Nang's gentle touch, was once again threatening to erupt. "What the *fuck* am I doing, standing here listening to you?"

"That Sings is really many songs, Chandler," Kee Nang said quickly, continuing to massage his chest. She feared she had revealed, said, too much already, but she could not think of anything else to do but continue. "We—this experience we call our universe—is but one of many songs. But there are only three songs that are of importance to you and me at the moment. We—humans in our universe—can be thought of as a kind of middle song. The Golden Children come from the highest song, or dimension. The creatures that attack Golden Children come from the lowest. In our song, our world, we are capable of experiencing and committing both good and evil. The song of Golden Children is pure good; the creatures' song is pure evil. These dimensions bleed together, if you will—different songs heard by different singers—only when Golden Children are sent to us, and the phenomenon lasts only so long as they live. It is during these periods that many legends are made, and religious myths born. But, you see, it has nothing to do with religion, as I have constantly told you. It is just something that happens—every thousand years."

"Why?" Chandler asked through lips that felt as stiff as leather.

"*Why?* Why what?"

"Why does it happen?"

"I don't know. Why do trees grow? Why does anything happen?"

"That's no answer."

"Precisely the point; there is no answer. That Sings does not send Golden Children to our song to help us, for the songs of evil—evil, that is, to us—are but other songs. That Sings is all songs, but the *Gompen Tarma* comes to us so that we may preserve our song."

"Then, this That Sings must care about us."

"No. That Sings does not care; That Sings *is* care, just as it is everything else."

"Then why does it send Golden Children to us in the first place?"

"Nobody knows."

"I don't see the point."

"Yes."

"Yes?"

"That's the point."

"*What's* the point?"

"That there is no point."

Chandler smiled gently. "Do you know that we sound like Abbott and Costello?"

"I don't understand what you mean."

"Never mind. All this is what you believe?"

"Yes."

"It still sounds like religion to me."

"No. All religions are basically the same— prescriptions for living combined with supernatural sanctions which will be applied if one does not follow the prescription. What I have given you is a description of reality which we Tibetans—and others—have found useful in explaining what we observe, and certain things we can do, such as dream transmission. But the Golden Child—and the creatures—are not descriptions of reality; they *are* real."

Chandler was silent, thinking, for some time. "I have a question," he said at last.

Kee Nang smiled. "Good grief. Only one?"

"The only important one, at least to me," Chandler said, grim-faced. "Your friendly neighborhood librarian said that nothing in this world could harm this Golden Child."

"That is true."

"What if they *deprive* him of something in this world?"

"Like what?"

"Like food. Can they starve him to death?"

Kee Nang's smile vanished. "I don't know. I will have to ask Kala. Is that what they're doing, Chandler? Are they starving the *Gompen Tarma?*"

Chandler did not reply. Sirens could now be heard in the distance, coming from many directions, converging on them. He abruptly pushed off the wall and walked quickly back up the alley, turned right at the juncture of the larger alley and headed for the street.

Kee Nang walked a few paces behind the Chosen One, noting that his stride was now steady and his hands had stopped shaking. She had done everything she could do, Kee Nang thought. His question about the possibility of starving the *Gompen Tarma* had disturbed her deeply. Also, she would have liked to question him about the content of all his dreams, and especially about Sardo Numspa, but she knew that she had already risked a great deal by telling him about dream transmission, That Sings, and the many dimensions of existence. She did not regret speaking to him of these things, for the Chosen One had been teetering on the brink of an abyss within his own mind and her words had pulled him back—at least for a time. But she did not want to press him.

She watched the back of the Chosen One, knew that the battle inside the soul of this tough but gentle man had now been fully joined. And the fate of the song heard by more than five billion people hung in the balance.

Chapter Thirteen

His nightmares were becoming even more vivid, Chandler thought as he surveyed the dream-vista around and below him, and he was just going to have to learn to be patient, not panic, and wait for them to end. He was still not certain he believed in dream transmission, or anything else Kee Nang had told him, but the conversation had served to ease his terror, and so he had decided to pay close attention to the images and words that came to him in his sleep. As far as he was concerned, he had nothing to lose. If he was insane, then . . . well, he was insane. But if he was not, if there was even the slightest possibility that the little boy existed and was being held . . .

Chandler found that he had come to love the child in—of—his dreams.

In what appeared to be a back room of the warehouse Chandler had visited in his dreams before, the reddish-haired, sinister-eyed man sat cross-legged, facing a bare wall. The man crossed his arms over his chest, and suddenly his hair began to blow backward, as if a ferocious wind were blowing from the wall. Suddenly the wall began to shimmer and glow, then melted away. Flame shot into the room, engulfing the man, but when the flame abruptly receded, the dark-eyed man was unscathed; not even his elegant suit had been singed. Beyond the wall there stretched a hellish landscape of fiery torment; the terrible wind carried howls of agony and terror up from lakes of blood and fire. In the foreground was a mountain, and cut into the side of the mountain was a cave.

Good show, Chandler thought. Send in the clowns.

Something inside the cave stirred, then spoke.

"Congratulations. You have the child."

The thing spoke in stereo, Chandler thought. Really good show.

"Thank you, Lord," Sardo Numspa replied, bowing his head slightly.

There was a prolonged silence, during which Numspa sat perfectly still while the wind blew, and the fiery lakes of blood boiled. Finally, with just a hint of annoyance, the thing in the cave spoke again.

"But he is still alive."

"You have no reason to fear him. He is surrounded at all times, in all directions, by evil."

"Do not underestimate the power of good in that song. Do not dismiss the strength of this child. Time grows short. The child will never eat the blood."

"What must I do, Lord?"

"First, move the child again before they discover where you are holding him."

"And to kill him?"

"The Ajanti dagger. It is not of that song. With it you could kill the child."

"It is well guarded. How can I get it?"

"Offer to exchange the child for it. They can refuse nothing for his safe return. When you have the knife, come to me. I will tell you how to use it to kill the child. We will use the Chosen One."

"Thank you, Lord."

"The Chosen One is with us now. Take him."

The wind stopped howling, and suddenly the hellish vista was gone; the wall was back in place. Sardo Numspa got to his feet, slowly turned—and pointed directly at Chandler.

Suddenly Chandler was falling. He hit the floor hard at Sardo Numspa's feet; pain shot through his elbow, and the wind was knocked out of him.

Something was very wrong, Chandler thought; the pain and breathlessness was new. In his dreams up to this point he had experienced only vague sensations of heat and cold, never anything like this. There was nothing vague about the sensations he was experiencing now: he *hurt*. Also, he had never felt so corporeal, so *real*. He looked down at his body, found that he was barefoot, dressed in the sweatpants and T-shirt he had worn to bed.

He heard a door open behind him. Chandler turned his head, was startled to see the monkey man and the giant enter. He started to say something, bit it off; he did not feel like making funny remarks. Indeed, he did not feel like talking at all, for he was certain that now he would hear his own voice, as well as those of the others.

He was no longer confident that this was a dream.

He was afraid.

No, he thought. He must not be afraid; he must fight the madness.

Or, if he was not mad, he must simply—fight. He had to use what he had learned from Kee Nang. He would assume that dream transmission was real, and that what was happening was possible on a mental plane; his mind was in touch with the child's captors, but his body was not endangered. The pain was an illusion. His consciousness might be floating about someplace, but his body was safely home in bed; his doors were locked, and his burglar alarm was set. Actual physical transport of the body was impossible.

The pain was an illusion; he was only *dreaming* of pain.

He would not be afraid. He would fight for control of his dream, struggle to find a way to turn it back on them.

Finally, he caught his breath. He got to his feet, turned his back on the giant and the monkey man. Looking directly into the face of the man in the fine suit and cape, he saw absolutely nothing remarkable about it. Indeed, the man was far more attractive than any of his companions, with features which vaguely reminded Chandler of an Italian count, as portrayed by an Italian actor in an Italian film. He had a thin, aquiline nose, thin lips. His eyes were pools of black oil; bright, intelligent. His hair was longish and thick, razor cut.

"Mr. Jarrell," Numspa said in a deep, pleasant voice as he stepped closer to Chandler. "It's good to see you. Thanks for dropping in."

"Speak for yourself," Chandler replied, and— although he had anticipated it—was startled by the sound of his own voice.

Don't be afraid; fear cripples. Fight; fight for control.

"I'm sure you're wondering why I've brought you here this evening."

Something smelled. It was a terrible, wet-animal smell. Chandler wheeled around, was startled to find the monkey man, steel whip coiled around his chest, standing so close that Chandler could smell his fetid, fecal, breath. The giant stood just behind him.

"Get those creeps out of here!" Chandler shouted, wheeling back to face the man in the gray suit.

"Of course," Numspa said easily. "Til, Fu; please leave us now."

Chandler turned his head and watched the giant and the monkey man walk out of the room, after casting hostile glances at him.

"Who the hell are you?" Chandler asked as he turned back to the man.

"My name is Sardo Numspa," the man replied in the same, easy tone.

"How come you're out of costume?"

"Excuse me?"

"Forget it. Just trying to inject a little levity into the proceedings."

"You seem remarkably sanguine for a man in such a particularly perilous situation."

"Bullshit. This dream is as much mine as yours. You can't hurt me, any more than I can hurt you."

Something moved in the man's dark eyes, and he raised his eyebrows slightly. "Is that what you think this is, Mr. Jarrell? Just a dream?"

"I know it is. You're missing one of your buddies, you know. Tommy Tong lost his head over this business."

The man smiled. "That is very witty, Mr. Jarrell. Yes, I know Tommy is dead. I killed him."

"You?"

"Yes."

"Why?"

"You would have forced Tommy to provide you with information which I didn't want you to have at the time."

"At the time?"

"It appeared that you were about to self-destruct from your own inner conflicts concerning the Golden Child. That would have been to my advantage, obviously, and I did not wish Tommy to verify this alternate reality. Also, of course, I did not want you coming for the Golden Child before I was ready for you."

"If you're referring to that business about a kid being sent every thousand years to bring good to us, I still don't believe that."

The man threw back his head and laughed. "That's good, Mr. Jarrell; just simply marvelous. This is indeed a very special age, especially in this part of your song which is called the West. The decision to bring the child to this city called Los Angeles was a sound one. But, in any case, the woman told you certain things which you are now prepared to accept as truth, and this has armed you in new ways. In truth, I now believe I made a mistake in killing Tommy. I should have let you put a gun to his head and force the truth out of him. I don't think you would have believed him, and it could have pushed you over the edge. In any case, it couldn't have been more harmful to my interests than what the woman found to say to you. You are much stronger now. Thus, there is no longer any reason for this . . . negotiation . . . not to take place."

"If I'm such a threat to you, why not kill me?"

"Because I need you to help me kill the *Gompen Tarma*."

"Lots of luck, pal. I'm telling you I'll find the kid. I'll find him in reality, not some stupid dream. And when I do, pal, I'm going to kill you, assuming you're still hanging around."

"I'll look forward to our final confrontation with great anticipation," the man said evenly.

"You've got the kid here, right?"

"Right."

"Where is this place? Tell me, and I'll drive around to see you when I wake up."

"Really? I thought you didn't believe in any of this, Mr. Jarrell."

"I've got nothing better to do."

"How do you feel now, Mr. Jarrell?"

"Like shit. This Chosen One gig can be a real bummer."

"But does this situation, this place . . . do I . . . seem real to you? Can you feel your breathing, your heart beating? Perhaps your elbow hurts where you hit it on the floor. Yes?"

Yes, Chandler thought. Fight the fear. It's your dream too. Don't let him control it.

"I guess that just means I'm getting really good at this dreaming shit, Sardi."

"Sardo."

"Sorry. I got you confused with the restaurant. Do you mind if I call you Sardi, Sardo? You can call me Mr. Jarrell."

Again, shadows moved in the man's eyes, and Chandler felt a tightening in his belly.

"You will call me Master, Mr. Jarrell."

"Not today, Sardi."

"For eternity. When the child dies, the song that is your world will end."

"I've got a big day ahead of me tomorrow, Sardi, looking for you. I'd appreciate it if we could get this over with so I can get a good night's sleep. What do you want?"

"I want to make you a very attractive offer."

"No shit? Let me tell you, I can really use a very attractive offer right now."

"Has it ever occurred to you how many men of less worth than yourself obtain so many of the riches of living, while you, who can imagine so much, have so little?"

"Damn; you've been reading my mail."

"What?"

"You're right. I think about the injustice of it all the time."

"Good. If you'll consent to serving me, I'm willing to give you power, position . . . whatever women you may desire. If you will agree to serve me, I will allow the song that is your world to remain for the rest of your lifetime, so that you may enjoy these things."

"Thanks, Sardi."

"Sardo."

"It's a hell of an offer, no pun intended, but all my friends will tell you that I'm heavily imbued with the Protestant Work Ethic. I'm not sure I could handle all that wine and all those women in any song."

"What?!"

"You're not a very quick fellow, Sardi. Do all demons lack a sense of humor, or is it just you?"

The man remained silent, staring at Chandler, for some time. His eyes appeared to be changing slightly, almost imperceptibly. Chandler heard footsteps behind him, smelled the fecal odor of the monkey man. He turned, watched the monkey man and the giant walk across the room, stop when they were flanking him. The monkey man, two feet shorter than Chandler, stared up into Chandler's face, and his leathery, simian lips parted in a malevolent smile that revealed broken, rotting teeth.

"I thought I told you to send these creeps to their rooms, Sardi," Chandler continued.

"I don't like your attitude," the man said in a tone of voice that was flat and ominous.

"Tough shit. If you don't like it, go dream with somebody else next time."

"I will repeat my offer one last time."

"Go fuck yourself, Sardi."

"I can see there's no use trying to talk to you."

"Thank goodness, no pun intended. If I were you, I'd toss me out of this dream right now."

"Til, please assist me."

There was danger in this very wrong dream, Chandler thought as the giant suddenly stepped behind him, grabbed both his arms, straightened and twisted them, forcing Chandler to bend over. His body was home in bed; it had to be. His body could not be there, even though his arms felt as if they were about to be pulled from their sockets.

Pain.

There shouldn't be pain in a dream, Chandler thought. But there was. A great deal of pain.

Chandler lifted his head to look at the man in the suit, and almost screamed. The eyes of his captor had changed from black to red on red, flaming pupils burning in pools of blood that were very large, extending from his temples to his cheekbones. The man's mouth opened, and a long, forked tongue flicked out and touched Chandler's forehead. Chandler winced and groaned through clenched teeth. There was an intense burning sensation, like acid, on the flesh of his forehead where the forked tongue had touched.

"How am I doing now, Mr. Jarrell?" the man continued in a voice that was like the hissing of a snake. "Do you like this costume? What do you think of my sense of humor now? Why aren't you laughing?"

Don't scream. Fight for control of the dream—before muscles tear and bones break.

"Fuck . . . you, Sardi."

"Oh? Would you like another kiss?"

". . . No."

"What is my name?"

"Sar . . . do."

"I am willing to make an exchange, Mr. Jarrell. I will trade the boy for the Ajanti dagger."

"Fuck you, Sardi."

Chandler could no longer keep his head up under the relentless pressure the giant was exerting on his arms. He groaned, bowed his head. Staring at the floor, he watched as English riding boots with gold spurs walked past him, to his right, then choked off a scream as something that looked like a slimy, scaled claw descended into his line of vision.

Then he did scream as the tip of the claw cut into the flesh of his forearm. He turned his head as far to the right as he could, saw blood dripping on the floor, felt its liquid warmth running down his arm. The giant pushed him forward, and he fell to the floor.

Chandler shook his head, started to cradle his bleeding right forearm, stopped when he saw the drawing of a strange, four-bladed dagger that had been carved there. He glanced up, found that the man's eyes were once again normal-sized, limpid pools of black; his face was once again that of an Italian count.

"Well, Mr. Jarrell, do you have anything to say now?"

Chandler remained silent, trying to fight back the mindless terror growing in him. His arm and forehead burned like fire hot enough to eat into bone, into soul.

"What's the matter, Mr. Jarrell? Cat got your tongue?"

"You're not real," Chandler managed to say in a hoarse voice. "None of this is real."

"No?" The man's mouth opened and the forked tongue flicked out, stopping a fraction of an inch from Chandler's eyes. "How about a kiss on the cheek? The lips?"

". . . No."

"Ah. Of course not." The man pointed to the dagger carved into Chandler's forearm. "A little something for you to remember me by, Mr. Jarrell. And I think you will remember me for a very long time, won't you?"

Chandler said nothing. There was too much terror, and he knew he had lost. Was lost.

"You must excuse me for a few minutes, Mr. Jarrell," the man continued, then turned to the giant. "Til, see that Mr. Jarrell doesn't make a nuisance of himself while I'm gone. As for you, Mr. Jarrell, when you have obtained the Ajanti dagger, I will contact you about the exchange." He paused, flicked his forked tongue, and once more his eyes expanded to huge pools of red on red. "Tell your lovely lady friend that Sardo Numspa sends his greetings."

Chandler watched as the man walked quickly from

the room; the monkey man, loping along with his curious, hopping stride, left with him. Chandler collapsed to the floor, rolling up into a ball and cradling his bleeding arm—and tried to think. Out of the corner of his eye he could see the giant staring at him.

It certainly all seemed painfully real enough, to say the least, Chandler thought. It also seemed that he was not going to wake up while he was in this place, at least not of his own accord . . . if he was ever going to wake up at all. What to do . . . ?

Try again to fight for control. And if he couldn't win mentally, then he would have to accept the conditions of the dream and try to do it physically.

"Oh, my God," he moaned loudly, then covered his face with his hands and started to sob.

Still sobbing, he struggled to his feet and began to stagger around in circles. He gradually straightened his course and angled in the direction of the door. Through the gaps in his fingers he watched as the huge Til, not unexpectedly, came across the room to block his path. Til seemed uncertain, and he bent down slightly in order to try to look into Chandler's face. Chandler continued to stagger forward until he was about to bump into the giant, then abruptly kicked with all his might into the man's groin.

Chandler was pleased to find that he was not the only one who could be hurt in this dream. Stunned, his eyes glazing over with pain and the breath exploding from his lungs, Til slowly sank to his knees, both his hands clutching his groin. Chandler nodded to him and smiled grimly just before bringing his knee up into the man's face. Like a great tree, the giant slowly toppled to the floor, and was unconscious.

Chandler searched the man's clothing for some kind

of weapon. There was none, and he rose and walked quickly to the door.

As he stepped out into the corridor, he idly wondered, smiling thinly at the thought, what would happen in this dream if he were to find his way out of this place, walk home, go to bed and fall asleep . . .

But before trying to escape from the building, he had to look for the Golden Child; to find the boy in his dream just might be the key to doing the same thing when he was awake . . .

His arm had stopped bleeding, but the wound, like the spot on his forehead, still burned. There were no windows in the room, and there were no windows in the narrow corridor he walked down. He turned right, started down another corridor. He came to a door, listened, but could hear nothing on the other side. He turned the knob, cautiously opened the door—and started in alarm.

Kee Nang was chained to the opposite wall. Her body sagged from exhaustion, and blood dripped from her wrists where shackles had cut into the flesh.

"Kee Nang!"

The woman's head slowly came up. She saw him, smiled sadly. "I'm sorry, Chandler," she whispered. "You must escape from this place."

"Jesus Christ, this is really an All Star production," Chandler said as he rushed across the room to her. "Kee Nang, are you really here?!"

"Run, Chandler."

He lifted the woman in his arms to ease the pressure of the shackles on her wrists, looked around the room for a key or some tool he could use to free her. There was nothing. "How the hell can I get you down from there?!"

"You can't. Leave me, Chandler. The Golden Child is here somewhere; find him, and escape."

"*Can* I escape?! And if I take the boy with me, will he be with me in real time?!"

"This is real time, Chandler. Don't . . . know the answer to your question. Nothing like this has ever happened before. It . . . is more than a message. If you do not escape from this place, you will die."

"It's just a dream!"

"Not just a dream, Chandler. More than a dream, more than a message. You know, because you have felt great pain."

Chandler cradled her in his arm, winced when the shackles slipped on her wrist and he saw her raw wounds. "Help me, Kee Nang! Tell me what to do! What's happening?!"

"Can't . . . help. This has . . . never happened. We are both trapped on a special plane of existence. I'm sorry . . . I can't help. Sardo Numspa is too . . . powerful. You must escape."

"I don't give a shit if this plane is a piper cub or a jumbo jet! I'm not leaving without you! I love you!"

"And I love you, Chandler. But—"

"You cannot save the woman, Mr. Jarrell," Sardo Numspa said from behind Chandler.

Chandler, still supporting Kee Nang's weight with one arm, turned to face Sardo Numspa, the monkey man, the giant, and another man from the raiding party who carried a sword. Suddenly, with incredible speed, the steel whip in the monkey man's hand lashed out and wrapped around Chandler's ankle, yanked him from his feet. The man with the sword rushed forward, raised the sword and brought it slashing down toward Chandler's leg. Chandler freed his ankle from the whip

138

and rolled away just in time as the sword crashed against the stone floor, sending sparks flying.

"Since you are obviously so resourceful," Sardo Numspa continued, "I think it might be a good idea to clip your wings in order to slow you down a bit. Fu; his unmarked arm . . ."

Chandler screamed as the whip again lashed out, wrapped around his left wrist, pulled. The giant leaped forward and wrapped his arms around his chest, holding him in place as his left arm was extended outward. The raider with the sword stepped forward, raised the blade and—

Chandler awoke, screaming, to find himself looking at a patch of dappled sunlight on his bedroom wall. He lay very still for a long time, waiting for the terror of the nightmare to pass. Tears flooded his eyes, rolled down his cheeks.

He was going to call somebody to pick him up and take him to a mental hospital the moment he gathered enough strength to get up and get dressed, he thought.

The idea passed when he finally sat up, looked down and knew, finally and beyond any doubt, that no psychiatrist or hospital was going to be able to help him. There were very few people or things in this . . . song . . . which could help him.

His bedsheets were soaked with blood from the wound on his right forearm, where the outline of a four-bladed dagger had been carved. His forehead burned as if it had been splashed with acid, and he knew even before he got up and looked into the mirror to confirm it that there would be a mark left there by the forked tongue of Sardo Numspa, a very serious demon, indeed.

So he really did have a bit of a problem, Chandler

thought as he gazed out his bedroom window at his eucalyptus trees swaying gently in a light morning breeze. Kee Nang had been telling the truth all along. About everything.

The world will become hell . . .
What you believe is irrelevant . . .
The dimensions of existence bleed together . . .
You are the Chosen One . . .
This song will cease to exist . . .

The day before, all he'd had to worry about was losing his mind. Now, it seemed, he had to worry about losing the world.

Chapter Fourteen

"It is the Ajanti dagger," Dr. Hong said in a strained voice as he stared at the carved image on Chandler's forearm. He paused, looked up at Chandler. "It has great power. This is what he wants in exchange for the child?"

"That's what he said," Chandler replied as he looked at Kee Nang, who stood close beside him in the dingy back room of the herb shop. She had her arm wrapped in his, and now she reached up and gently touched the mark on his forehead, which had already turned to milky, puckered scar tissue. To his right, the half-naked woman behind the scrim was breathing heavily.

"So," Kala rasped in her eerie, rustling voice, "it is Sardo Numspa we must deal with. There is no record of his ever having ascended this high before. There must be a special reason."

"He told me he believed he could destroy the world forever this time," Chandler said quietly. "Reading between the lines, I think he believes this age we live in is particularly vulnerable—possibly because I refused to believe." Chandler paused, smiled wryly. "Since he considers me such a lousy Chosen One, he's decided to up the ante."

Kee Nang frowned. "But you believe now."

Chandler grunted, looked down at the mark on his forearm; it, too, had quickly scarred, but the puckered tissue was blood red. "Oh, yeah," he said in a flat voice. "Old Sardo sure enough did make a believer out of me. But I don't think it's changed his opinion of me, or his plans; he still believes he can destroy us forever."

"Then he risks his own destruction," Kala rasped.

"You will defeat him, Chandler," Kee Nang said, squeezing his arm. "You will save the *Gompen Tarma*, and that will defeat him."

Chandler caught a look on Dr. Hong's face which clearly indicated that the old man did not share Kee Nang's confidence: his flesh was ashen, and there was a haunted look in his eyes.

"Sardo Numspa," Kala said to no one in particular. "This is terrible."

"What's this knife?" Chandler asked Kee Nang.

It was Kala who answered. "The dagger of Ajanti was hammered in the lowest song from one hundred million souls of the tormented in other songs. It took four thousand years to make, and the labor of all the creatures of that lowest plane. It was originally brought to this world to kill the second *Gompen Tarma*, a bearer of justice. His death was a great loss, and its effect has rippled through the ages; it is why, today, so many of the innocent suffer, and terrible crimes go unpunished."

Kee Nang touched the outline on Chandler's arm. "It is what you Americans call a double-edged sword. It has four blades, and cuts in all directions. There is no one it cannot kill."

"Will it kill Numspa?"

"Yes," Kala answered, "but you must not even think of pitting yourself against him in that manner, Chandler Jarrell. Your mission—and the only thing you can possibly accomplish—is to rescue the *Gompen Tarma*. You must obtain the dagger, and then trick Numspa into freeing the *Gompen Tarma;* but you must not let him get possession of the knife."

"Is that all?" Chandler said distantly. A thought was trying to form in the back of his mind; he reached for it, but it eluded him. "How am I supposed to do that?"

"I don't believe you can," Hong said in a tortured voice. "Kala, it may prove necessary to actually exchange the dagger for the *Gompen Tarma.*"

"That doesn't sound like such a hot idea," Chandler said, still pursuing the thought which slipped away like quicksilver each time he approached it. "The knife can kill the boy."

"I agree," Kee Nang said tersely. "Chandler, it will be up to you to trade for the *Gompen Tarma*—without making the actual trade."

Chandler shook his head, abandoning his forced pursuit of the elusive idea. "Where is this Ajanti dagger?"

"In Tibet," Kee Nang replied. "It is kept in the temple of Karma Tang." She paused, glanced at Dr. Hong. "But there is no guarantee that the Abbot will let us have it."

Chandler looked back and forth between the woman and the old man. "If you think it's necessary to have the dagger in order to save the child, why wouldn't he let you have it?"

"Because he might not agree," Kee Nang answered. "The Abbot of Karma Tang is . . . a very difficult man. There is never a way of knowing in advance what he will do about anything."

There was a prolonged period of silence which Chandler felt pressing on his heart like a physical force. Finally he nodded over his shoulder, toward the curtained entrance and the corridor beyond, with its paintings. "The picture out there: that's what Sardo Numspa really looks like?"

Kee Nang nodded. "That is his real form."

"Christ, he's an ugly sucker. No wonder he's so cranky. I'll bet all the other little demons down there picked on him when he was a kid."

Dr. Hong's mouth dropped open in shock, but Kee Nang laughed lightly—and the tension of the depressing silence was finally broken. "You can so easily make jokes about that thing after what it has done to you? Chandler, you have no fear!"

"Wrong. I have plenty of fear. I was simply pointing out the fact that he is one ugly sucker. Don't you agree?"

Kee Nang laughed again, nodded. "I agree. Sardo Numspa is one ugly sucker."

Kala rasped, "He is the most vicious of the creatures in the lowest song."

Instantly, the tension returned.

"We will sacrifice whatever need be for the *Gompen Tarma*, Mr. Jarrell," Dr. Hong said gravely. "If we have to give up the Ajanti dagger, then we will.

Tomorrow, you must leave with Kee Nang for Tibet to obtain the dagger."

Once again, the thought flitted through Chandler's mind; this time he grabbed for and caught it, pinned it down, looked at it squarely. "I don't think so," he said.

He watched Hong and Kee Nang exchange startled, anxious glances. It was the old man who spoke.

"You won't do this for the *Gompen Tarma?* You *must,* Mr. Jarrell. It is our consensus."

"Consensus? Who's the Chosen One?"

"You are, Chandler," Kee Nang said softly, without hesitation.

"Precisely. And it's because I'm the Chosen One that I don't think I'm going to Tibet. Consider: both of you, and Kala in particular, have shown considerable consternation over the fact that I ended up the Chosen One in this thousand year cycle. You would have much preferred somebody from the East, or maybe even a garden-variety guru from Malibu—somebody, anybody, who wouldn't have taken so much convincing, and given you such a hard time. Well, maybe That Sings, this force you talk about, had a reason—"

"For making you the Chosen One?" Kee Nang interrupted. "Your reasoning is incorrect, Chandler, precisely because That Sings does not reason. You are the Chosen One simply . . . because you are the Chosen One."

"But I *am* the Chosen One; since I am, maybe the means to rescue the child and defeat Numspa lies *here,* in *this* culture. And the *kid* is here, in Los Angeles. We don't have a whole lot of time; the kid's running out of leaves."

Dr. Hong frowned, shook his head. "Leaves?"

Chandler turned toward the scrim and the backlit

shadow of a woman. "Kala? Can the Golden Child be starved to death in this song?"

The answer came at once. "Yes."

"Then one of two things is going to happen very soon," Chandler said curtly, turning back to face Kee Nang and Dr. Hong. "Either he's going to die of starvation, or he's going to end up too weak to resist eating some of that bloodied oatmeal. I don't care where he comes from, or what else he means to you: to me, beyond all else, he's a five-year-old boy. He's a brave little boy, the gutsiest I've ever seen—but he's still a little boy. I'm telling you that little kid is scared, lonely—and goddam hungry. So I'm not about to traipse off to Tibet on a wild-dagger chase when the kid's right here, suffering and hoping, and counting on me to find him. Sardo Numspa may be right about this being a vulnerable age spiritually, but they sure as hell didn't have cars, helicopters, SWAT teams and the F.B.I. a thousand years ago. I've got enough pull with the police department to get an all-points bulletin put out for the boy, Sardo Numspa and his whole ugly crew, without too many questions being asked up front. Then we'll see how those sons-of-bitches match up against an L.A.P.D. SWAT team. You say the boy can't be harmed anyway, as long as he remains pure, so we don't have to worry about him being hit by a stray bullet. I'd like to see how Numspa and his menagerie react when they get their first whiff of good old twentieth-century tear gas."

All the time he had been speaking, Kee Nang and the old Chinese had been slowly shaking their heads in unison, like a mute Greek chorus.

"Your words are powerful yet sweet, Chandler, and they come from deep in your heart," Kee Nang said, fear and anxiety moving in the dark pools of her eyes. "But you are wrong. You don't seem to understand that bullets and tear gas will have no effect on Sardo Numspa."

"So what? Bullets will damn well tear up the others, and I can get to the boy while Numspa is busy doing magic tricks for the cops."

"No, Chandler." There was now a faint, bell-tone of desperation in the woman's voice. "You must listen to us. The police will never be able to find Sardo Numspa and the *Gompen Tarma;* only you can do that. You will be wasting precious time if you count on any authority but yourself to search. To continue that search, it is now necessary to get the Ajanti dagger."

"Fine. No problem. You go get the dagger, and I'll take care of business in my own way on this end. Then, if the police and F.B.I. come up empty, we'll have the dagger to trade."

"I can't get the dagger, Chandler," Kee Nang said in a small voice. Her face, like Hong's, had gone very pale. "Only the Chosen One can obtain the Ajanti dagger—assuming that the Abbot of Karma Tang will permit the attempt."

"Attempt?"

"The Ajanti dagger is not something one picks up at a local sporting goods shop, Chandler. You will understand, eventually—I hope."

"Why can't the Abbot give *you* permission?"

"You will see. You *must* come with me, Chandler. *Please.* Now you believe, know that everything I have told you is the truth."

"This has nothing to do with the things you've told me. Dr. Hong mentioned a consensus; that makes this a judgment call."

"You are right when you say it is a 'judgment call'; you are wrong if you judge that it is not necessary to try to get the Ajanti dagger. You and I must go to Tibet."

Chandler breathed deeply, drew himself up straight. He looked into the faces of Kee Nang and Dr. Hong, glanced at the still shadow of Kala, remembered the smiling face of the hungry little boy. "How do any of you know that Sardo Numspa isn't just trying to trick us into wasting time by going to Tibet while the boy continues to starve and grow weaker?" He paused, waited, but there was no reply. "Right: you can't be certain. How good an idea can it be if it came from Sardo Numspa?"

"It is a forced move, Chandler," Kee Nang whispered.

"Well, let me tell you something; I may not be any great shakes as a Chosen One, but I seem to be the only one we've got—and I may be the last we'll ever have. Since the boy is ultimately my responsibility, I'll make the final decision as to what we do, and where we go. I'll let you know what it is."

Kee Nang and Hong exchanged glances, and then Hong bowed slightly to Chandler.

"Could you please leave us for a moment?"

Chandler shrugged, turned and walked out through the curtain.

"Kee Nang," Hong said in a trembling voice as he gently gripped the woman's arms. "I may have no right . . . but a way must be found to get the Chosen One to go to Tibet." He paused, lowered his gaze and his voice. "No price is too great to pay."

"I agree," Kee Nang whispered, then bowed her head as tears welled in her eyes.

Chapter Fifteen

CHANDLER STOOD AT ONE END OF THE SHOP, ABSENTLY staring down at the contents of a glass case. Inside were what appeared to be dried seahorses, antelope hooves, snake skins . . .

"Yak loin. Good to keep the yang up."

"Huh?" Startled, Chandler looked up into the smiling face of a clerk. He had not heard the man come up.

The clerk made an obscene gesture with his fingers. "Yang; yak loin keep it up."

"That, I don't need," Chandler said with a thin smile as he thought of Kee Nang—and his nagging desire for her even amid the nightmare that his life had become. "You got anything to keep it down?"

The clerk merely shrugged, walked away. Chandler glanced to his left, where a small old woman stood examining the herbs in the case. "Try the yak loin on your husband," Chandler continued in a confidential whisper, leaning toward the woman. "It's going to make you a very happy woman."

"I'm already a happy woman," she replied evenly, in perfect English.

"Oh," Chandler said, feeling thoroughly rebuffed. "Well, try it anyway."

Kee Nang suddenly emerged from the curtain, mouth set in a grim line. Chandler turned toward her inquiringly, but she walked past without looking at him. "Come, Chandler," she said in a tense voice, "I will take you home now."

They rode in strained silence out of Chinatown, through Los Angeles, to Chandler's modest hilltop home. Kee Nang pulled up to the curb on the street at the foot of the hill. Chandler opened the door and started to get out, was stopped by the sound of Kee Nang's voice.

"Aren't you going to invite me up, Chandler?"

Chandler turned back, found that he was immediately aroused. The woman, with her oval face, long black hair, limpid black eyes, and firm breasts beneath her white sweatshirt, had never looked more beautiful or desirable to him.

And somewhere in the city of night a child was hungry, lonely, and waiting for him, while the world as he knew it teetered on the edge of oblivion.

"Why now?" he asked tightly.

Kee Nang cocked her head, smiled uncertainly. "Are you turning me down?"

"I'm asking why now?"

"Because I am afraid," the woman answered simply.

"Afraid that I'm not going to fly off to Tibet to look for this dagger?"

Kee Nang flushed, quickly looked away for fear that Chandler would see the truth in her eyes. "Is it so bad for me to suggest that we both seek solace and sanctuary from our fears for a few hours in each other's arms?"

Chandler reached out, took the woman's hand and helped her from the car.

He had been turgid from the moment Kee Nang had suggested they make love, and didn't imagine that he could become any more aroused. He'd been wrong, he thought, as he lay on the bed, watching as the naked Kee Nang, standing at the foot of the bed, removed the four jeweled pins she always wore in her hair. Her body seemed flawless—or at least it was everything Chandler had always considered erotically perfect and desirable in a body. He had never suffered from premature ejaculation before, but he feared he was about to.

"I know you are anxious to put your hands on me," Kee Nang said in a small voice as she removed the last pin from her hair. "If you'll wait just a few moments more, I believe I can enhance our pleasure."

Chandler watched, bewildered, as Kee Nang stuck a pin on each of the four walls of the bedroom. As the last pin was put in place, the jeweled heads of all four began to glow with their respective gem colors. As Kee Nang walked toward the bed, the intensity of the gems' glow increased, bursting out and filling the room with a soft nimbus that warmed Chandler and made his flesh feel as if it were being gently caressed with fine silk.

"What the *hell* is going on?"

"Just a little 'magic trick' for us," Kee Nang said as

she got into bed next to Chandler, put her open mouth on his, reached under the sheet and began to stroke his body.

As he had feared would happen, Chandler immediately ejaculated—or thought he did. What he experienced was a spasmodic shudder that rippled through his body, and which certainly *felt* like an orgasm. There was the sensation of ejaculation, but there was no sudden drop in excitement or onset of fatigue. All of the excitement and arousal he had been feeling remained undiminished. And he continued to experience a sensation of ejaculation.

"Good grief," Chandler murmured, hardly able to speak for all of the ecstatic sensations rippling through his body as he slowly entered Kee Nang.

"Wow," Chandler gasped, staring wide-eyed at the ceiling, basking in the warm, silken gem-glow which continued to suffuse the room. He was still hard, could still go on, but for a few minutes he simply wanted to hold the woman, talk with her. Love her in a different way. "Whatever it is that goes on with those pins, they sure as hell beat oysters."

Kee Nang, facing away from Chandler, fought against the hot tears that welled in her eyes and rolled down her cheeks. Self-pity, she thought. The man must never know. "You know what I would like now?" she asked quietly.

"Whatever it is you want, kiddo, you got it."

"I would like the Chosen One to tell me about himself."

Chandler felt a chill pass through him, but it was almost instantly chased by the ethereal gem-glow and the woman's touch. "Not much to tell, Kee Nang."

152

"Then tell me not much."

"Why do you want to hear depressing things? Nothing I have to tell you about myself is good."

The tears were gone. Kee Nang turned, propped herself up on one elbow and gazed thoughtfully into Chandler's face. "That can't be true, since *you* are so good. How did you come to start looking for missing children? Please share your past with me."

Chandler sighed, stroked the woman's hair. "I have good memories from when I was a small child. We were a family then—before my father started losing jobs and a few other things started to happen. You have to understand that the ghetto can crush anyone, even the strongest man or woman. I guess it finally crushed my father. He got into drugs, and those drugs stole his mind. He left when I was about seven years old, and I never saw him again. Then my mother—she became a drunk. She got run over by a truck outside some bar."

"Oh, Chandler," Kee Nang whispered, caressing his cheek with the back of her hand. "I'm so sorry."

"Yeah. But I got lucky—a lot luckier than my mother or father ever got. I was placed in a Catholic orphanage, and that was probably the best thing that ever happened to me. I was a good kid, I guess—which I like to think means that my Mom and Dad were good people. They just never had much of a chance in life."

"Yes, Chandler. That is true."

"I was never in much trouble, and I always did pretty good in school. Anyway, I was Valedictorian of my high school class, and I got a full scholarship to go to Syracuse University. I decided I wanted to be a social worker, to help people and give them—especially children—the kind of second chance I'd had. I used the scholarship to go to Syracuse's Maxwell School, one of the best schools for social work in the country. I transferred to U.S.C. in my junior year, even played some football. After graduation, I went to work for the city of Los Angeles.

"It didn't take me long to realize that I was going to be very frustrated in that job as a caseworker. Not that the city didn't—and doesn't—try hard to take care of people who need help, but it's really an impossible job. There are just too many people in need, and caseworkers are constantly bogged down in paperwork. You spend as much time shuffling files and pushing forms as you do working with people, and it gets so that the paperwork takes all your energy—it exhausts you, and keeps you from being as effective as you could be. Anyway, it took me three years to decide what I was going to do about my frustration. I still wanted to give children a second chance—but I wanted to *make a difference*. So I quit my job, got a private investigator's license . . . and here I am."

"Yes," Kee Nang said softly, gently kissing him on the cheek. "Here you are. Would you like to make love with me again?"

"Yes . . . after you tell me about the person I'm making love with. I already know you're a world-class martial artist, so you can skip over that part."

Kee Nang shrugged. "The martial arts were considered a part of my spiritual training, and I guess I do have some natural talent."

"I'd say so."

"As for the rest of it, I've experienced none of the suffering you have."

"You said your father left."

"Perhaps 'left' was not the correct word. He was not physically present to be with my mother and me like other husbands and fathers because of his religious duties, but he was always with us spiritually, and we always felt his love in our home. My mother and I adjusted.

"As you pointed out, I am most fortunate to come from a 'well-to-do' family; like you, I also happened to do well in school. I spent my early childhood years in Tibet, of course, but received intensive language training. I took my higher education in England. I have two doctorates from Oxford."

"No shit?"

"No."

"In what?"

"Physics and philosophy. I was doing post-doctoral work in quantum theory when . . . the Golden Child was taken, and the omens indicated that it was my destiny to come to you." Kee Nang paused, lowered her gaze slightly, ran her fingers across Chandler's chest. "Chandler," she continued at last, "in many ways I am as 'Western' as you—perhaps more so. You must believe me when I say that obtaining the Ajanti dagger is the best—perhaps only—hope for gaining the safe return of the Golden Child. The fact that you are the Chosen One has nothing to do with your culture, your background, or your belief system. It has to do with your heart. There is no 'East' or 'West' in the songs of existence. Our song is our song. Will you come with me to Tibet and the temple of Karma Tang?"

Chandler tensed slightly. "Is that what this lovemaking gig is all about . . . Doctor? To get me around to your way of thinking? Did you come to bed with me so you could manipulate me, Kee Nang?"

"I came to bed with you because I was afraid," Kee Nang replied evenly. Hurt swam in her eyes. "That is as

I told you. I also came to bed with you because it was something I very much wanted to do. I am going to Tibet whether you come or not; from here, I am driving directly to the airport. I am going because I know it must be done. For now, we have no choice but to play Sardo Numspa's game."

"I thought I was the only one who could get this dagger."

"As far as we know, that is true. In which case, I will die trying. There is simply no other way to save our song; if the *Gompen Tarma* dies, my death will be of no consequence."

Chandler sighed, looked up at the ceiling. "I guess it could be argued that I'm a bit new at this Chosen One business to be rejecting advice from people who should know what they're talking about."

"Each Chosen One has been new at the 'business,' Chandler. You must do what you think is best. So must I."

Kee Nang paused a moment to watch Chandler's anxious face.

"You must sleep for a while, Chandler," Kee Nang murmured, turning away as tears once again welled in her eyes. "You will need your strength."

Chandler had been very conscious of the tension inside the car as Dr. Hong had driven them to the airport; neither Hong nor Kee Nang had spoken a word, and the woman had a pale, haunted look. Now, waiting inside the crowded terminal, Chandler was tired of the silence. He set down their bags, gently took Kee Nang's elbow and turned her toward him.

"Kee Nang, is something wrong?"

"Of course not," the woman replied tersely, refusing

156

to meet his gaze. She pulled away from his grasp. "I'll get the tickets."

"You must not be angry with Kee Nang for trapping you into going," the ancient Chinese whispered in Chandler's ear as both men watched Kee Nang walk stiffly away.

Chandler felt an uncomfortable tightening in his stomach. He turned to face the other man, frowned. "What do you mean?"

"It was I who told her to do it."

"What do you *mean?*"

Hong slowly blinked. "She didn't tell you?"

"You tell me."

"Ah," Hong said, dropping his eyes. "Perhaps I shouldn't—"

"Tell me, Hong!" Chandler snapped. "What's wrong with Kee Nang?!"

Dr. Hong sighed deeply, continued to stare at the floor. "In our culture," he said in a low voice, "a woman may not give herself to any man but her husband. She can never marry now. She has given you what was most precious to her."

"How the hell do you know what's gone on between Kee Nang and me?"

"I know; it is written all over your face . . . and hers. When she gave you her body, she gave you her future. It was to obligate you, so that you would get the knife."

Chandler swallowed, found that his mouth was very dry. "What are you talking about? She's an educated woman, and this isn't the Dark Ages. No woman has to marry the first guy she spends a little time with. This is the twentieth century."

"Not for us."

"Yeah? What is it for you?"

Now the old man looked up; his gaze was steady on Chandler's face, his voice steady and strong. "Just another century."

"I don't get it," Chandler said, shaking his head. "You're telling me last night was just about the knife, and now she can't marry?"

Hong's silence was his answer. Chandler turned, stared across the terminal to where Kee Nang, chin high and back stiff, was waiting in the ticket line.

"But she must have known I'd go to get the knife," he continued in a hollow voice.

Now it was Hong who seemed surprised. "Then why would she . . . ? Now you are the only man . . ." Again, Hong dropped his gaze as Chandler looked at him. "I never should have spoken to you about this," he added quickly. "Only the Golden Child is important. Please don't—"

But suddenly he was talking to himself as Chandler snatched up the bags and hurried over to where Kee Nang was standing in line.

"Forgive me," Hong continued in a barely audible whisper as he closed his eyes and bowed his head in prayer. "I have sacrificed Kee Nang to bind the Chosen One to us. I felt it was necessary. If I was wrong in not having trusted the American, may I die . . . but may the *Gompen Tarma* be saved."

All through the long flight, Chandler had been very conscious of the haunted sadness in his silent, pale-faced companion—and he was not at all certain of what to do about it. He felt confused, fearful . . .

"That's beautiful," he said, pointing down to the soaring peaks they were passing over.

"Yes," Kee Nang said in a small voice, still staring

straight ahead of her. "Kathmandu is the gateway to Tibet. After we land, it will be two days into the mountains; then we will be at the heights of heaven."

"I want you to know I'm going to save the Golden Child."

"Of course you are," Kee Nang said in the same, small voice.

Chandler took a deep breath, turned in his seat to face Kee Nang. Now the words came pouring out of him. "In addition to that, I know you need to marry somebody . . . and I'm willing to do it. I'm the logical guy; hell, I'm the only guy. You're an okay woman, and you deserve a full life. So I'm willing to do it."

Kee Nang's reaction was not exactly what Chandler had been expecting. She suddenly stiffened in her seat as if an electric shock had gone through her, then abruptly turned to look at him. Her voice was no longer small, but cold—like her eyes. "You're asking me to marry you?"

"Uh, yeah," Chandler replied uncertainly, taken aback by the chill in Kee Nang's eyes and voice. "Consider it a proposal."

"You can't be serious." If anything, Kee Nang's voice had grown even colder.

"Will you marry me? There; that makes it an official proposal."

"What would ever make you think I would want to marry you?"

Chandler felt like a fist had landed in his stomach. He swallowed hard, licked his lips. "Well, uh, I thought . . . given your situation . . ."

"Dr. Hong told you." It was not a question.

"Uh, yeah. Hey, why *wouldn't* you marry me?"

"Because you are a distrustful egotist who gives no

consideration to the consequences of his actions," Kee Nang replied evenly, glaring at him. "You are a reckless fool who runs around thinking he knows everything about everything. Why would I want to marry a man like that?"

Deeply hurt, Chandler flushed angrily. "Yeah!" he snapped. "Why would you want to marry a man like that?!"

Kee Nang's response was to turn away, then buckle her seat belt in preparation for the descent.

The white van had been pulled into the main storage room of the warehouse. Til and the monkey man, taking care to stay well out of range of the *Gompen Tarma's* touch, threaded two poles through the bars of the evil cage, lifted it and slid it into the rear of the van. The doors were slammed shut; Til and Fu got into the cab, and the van rumbled out through the open doors of the warehouse.

In the gloom of the interior of the box of the van, the Golden Child, his expression passive and resigned, slowly removed the twig from inside the folds of his robe; there was only a single leaf left. The boy-child hesitated, then plucked this last leaf and slowly, almost reverentially, placed it in his mouth. . . .

Chapter Sixteen

KATHMANDU WAS, QUITE LITERALLY, BREATHTAKINGLY
cold—and beautiful; a fabled land at the bottom of an
ocean of clear, thin air bounded by the Himalayas.

Dressed in a Tibetan sheepskin jacket and fur-lined
cap, Chandler stood in the middle of a stone-paved
street, occasionally hopping up and down and beating
his arms against his body for warmth, as he waited for
Kee Nang to emerge from what she'd called a "trekking
office" up the street. Both sides of the narrow thor-
oughfare were lined with old, clay-brick buildings
which had stood for centuries, and which seemed
impervious to time, the thin air, and the bone-rattling
cold. At the far end of the street, visible as if through
the aperture of a square telescope, purple, blue and
white mountains rose into the sky, dwarfing all else and

filling Chandler with a sense of majesty, awe, and . . . humility.

Enough was enough, Chandler thought. Although he had purposely been exposing himself to the cold in an attempt to become acclimated, he had to get inside—even though he knew the cold would feel even more bitter when he emerged from the steamy heat he longed to find there. He started to walk back toward the trekking office, then suddenly stopped so quickly he almost tripped over his feet.

Behind him, a bird trilled a song that was almost painfully sweet and clear in the cold, thin air. It was an unmistakable song—one he had heard before, from the apparition that had appeared to him in his back yard.

Chandler spun around, and his breath caught in his throat when he saw the brilliantly plumed bird sitting on a branch of a tree between two buildings. He did not question the presence of the apparently tropical bird in the frigid clime of Kathmandu; he no longer questioned anything . . .

Suddenly the bird darted away, to Chandler's right. It flew up a side street, cut left into an alley.

Chandler looked back, but Kee Nang had not yet emerged from the trekking office. He could not wait; he sprinted up the side street, cut left into the alley where he had seen the bird disappear. He paused, looked all around him; the bird was nowhere in sight. Chandler groaned inwardly—not only at the apparent loss of the bird, but at the sight of an old, thinly clad and legless beggar sitting with his back braced against the wall of a building halfway up the alley. A battered tin alms-cup was clasped in an outstretched, trembling hand.

Chandler walked slowly up the alley, paused to drop a few coins in the beggar's cup, then went on to the end of the alley which opened into a circular courtyard which brought back unpleasant memories of the *cul-de-sac* where Tommy Tong had been decapitated.

There was no sign of the bird, no song . . .

Frustrated and suddenly depressed, Chandler turned and started back down the alley; he could not help but question now whether he had actually seen the bird at all. After all, he thought, the unrelenting cold and thin air could probably do things to a man's head.

But he knew this wasn't the case; he had not seen an apparition. The bird had been there, and then it had disappeared. Why had it appeared at all? He felt filled with an inexplicable sadness, and he hunched his shoulders against the cold and hung his head as he trudged slowly back up the alley.

He heard a faint rattling sound. He looked up and saw that the legless beggar, hearing his approaching footsteps, was once again holding out his tin alms-cup in one hand, a cheap tin trinket on a string in the other, and was banging the two objects together. Chandler stopped in front of the man, and was struck anew by how thinly clad the old man was; he wondered how the beggar could survive in the terrible cold. *He* was certainly cold, Chandler thought—but his cold must be nothing compared to the old beggar's. And he had his legs.

He also had a heavy coat, and could easily walk on his two legs to the main street a few yards away and buy another one . . .

Chandler removed his coat, bent down and draped it over the frail shoulders of the old beggar. He also put a bill in the cup, then started to walk away, wrapping his arms around his chest for warmth. He stopped when he heard a loud clanging behind him. He turned, saw that the legless beggar was banging his cup almost angrily on the stone walk, at the same time insistently holding out the tin medallion on a string. Chandler, who understood the demands of pride, went back and took the medallion from the man's trembling hand. He absently draped it around his neck, then hurried back down the alley.

Throughout the two-day trek, on mountain ponies across the border and up into the mountains of neighboring Tibet, he had become increasingly annoyed, then obsessed, with the cheap trinket hanging like an albatross around his neck. Time and again he would reach up and try to snap the thin string—but only managed to irritate the back of his neck. There was no knot in the string to untie and—although it had slipped easily enough over his head when he had first put it on—it now proved impossible to remove. He could not bite through it, and even knives and scissors proved no match for the eerie, otherworldly strength of the ordinary-looking string.

He'd mentioned the beggar to Kee Nang, shown her the problematical trinket. She had tried to cut it off, but had given up after one attempt.

Such things, Kee Nang had said, are perhaps better left alone.

Chandler found the mountains awesome, their indestructible grandeur filling him with a sense of eternity—and even peace. Somehow, the majestic, sweeping beauty of the temple of Karma Tang fit in with its surroundings beautifully. The journey, climaxed by their entrance into the great temple, had left Chandler in a kind of stupor, as if he had been drugged with the best that humankind and . . . That Sings . . . had to offer.

He was shocked out of his stupor when he saw the Abbot, walking slowly toward them through two rows of purple-robed monks from the far end of the great hall. The Abbot of Karma Tang wore purple and gold robes of the finest silk, but over his frail shoulders was draped the heavy sheepskin coat Chandler had given him when he was posing as a legless beggar in an alley in Kathmandu.

Chandler absently put his hand over the trinket hanging around his neck. It felt warm.

"Greetings, Father," Kee Nang said, bowing slightly as the Abbot joined them on the elevated vestibule just inside the entrace to the temple.

"Welcome, Daughter," the Abbot replied, raising her up and kissing her cheek. Then he turned to Chandler, and smiled. "Thank you for your coat, Mr. Jarrell. It has served me well."

"I'm glad you like it," Chandler said tersely. He felt foolish, as if he had been made the butt of some joke. "I'm also glad to see you've got your legs back. By the way, this necklace you gave me—"

"I didn't give it to you," the Abbot interrupted. His huge, almond-colored eyes danced with light. "You earned it."

"Whatever. It won't come off."

"Ah. You must be made of exceptionally strong, high-quality material."

Chandler flushed. *"I must be made—?!"*

"Why have you come here, Daughter?" the Abbot asked Kee Nang, abruptly turning away from Chandler.

Kee Nang glanced at Chandler, who could see that she was nervous. He nodded encouragement, and she looked back into her father's eyes. "Chandler is the Chosen One, Father."

"I know that."

"We . . . have come to ask for the sacred dagger of Ajanti."

"Ah," the old man breathed, and was then silent for long moments. At the mention of the dagger, Chandler thought he had heard an agitated rustling and murmur from the great chamber below the elevated vestibule; but when he looked to his right, all of the two hundred or so monks were kneeling in the same position, motionless. Finally, the Abbot asked: "For what reason?"

"It is for the *Gompen Tarma.*"

"He has no need of it," the Abbot replied evenly.

"It is to save his life, Father."

"It is for our sakes that the child lives, Kee Nang, not his own. I don't think it is a good idea for you to take the Ajanti dagger. The dagger should remain where it is, where it can do no harm. Other ways must be found to save the child, if he is to be saved. I refuse your request."

Which meant they had come to Tibet for nothing, Chandler thought as he caught Kee Nang's desperate look. Wasted days, a trip halfway around the world for nothing more than a family reunion, while a child was dying. No way he was going to let this happen.

"She's not the Chosen One," Chandler said curtly.

The old man slowly turned from his daughter to face Chandler directly. "That is true," he said quietly, intently studying Chandler's face.

"*I'm* the Chosen One."

"That is true."

"Out of five billion people on the face of this planet—in our song—I have been chosen to defend the Golden Child."

"That is true," the Abbot of Karma Tang said in the same soft, casual tone of voice.

"Well, *I'm* asking you for the dagger."

"Ah. And what do you, Chandler Jarrell, know of these things? What do you know of what the Ajanti dagger can and cannot do?"

"Nothing," Chandler replied evenly, matching the Abbot's steady gaze and tone of voice.

"Then what tells you that you should attempt to use the dagger in the child's rescue? Is it because Kee Nang has suggested this course of action?"

"No. My . . . heart tells me."

"Only a man whose heart is pure may wield the Ajanti dagger, Chandler Jarrell. It can easily kill its bearer."

"Then I could be in a lot of trouble," Chandler said evenly. "I can't say my heart is any purer than the next man's; in fact, it's probably a lot less pure. Still, I must have the dagger. Where is it?"

Chandler watched the Abbot and his daughter exchange glances. "It is not kept on this plane," the old man said, and touched the puckered, milky scar on Chandler's forehead.

There was a flash of light behind his eyes, a moment

of nausea, and the sound of a tiny, tinkling bell. Then Chandler suddenly found himself standing with Kee Nang and her father in a large room that glowed with light from some source which Chandler could not see. The room was totally bare; at the opposite end was a great set of iron-banded, wooden doors. Chandler felt virtually weightless.

"What have you done to me?" Chandler asked.

"I have brought you to the threshold of the Ajanti Journey," the Abbot replied evenly.

"Why in a dream?" Chandler asked, looking back and forth between Kee Nang and her father. "This isn't real; none of it feels real. How the hell am I supposed to bring something back from a dream?"

"This is not a dream, Chandler Jarrell," the Abbot said.

"This is not a dream, Chandler," Kee Nang said.

"It is a dream. I know the feeling."

"Did you bring this back from a dream?" the Abbot asked, touching the mark on Chandler's forehead. He then pointed to the mark on his forearm. "Did you bring that back from a dream?"

Chandler looked down at the scars on his forearm, felt the one on his forehead start to burn. "You have a point," he said quietly.

"Chandler," Kee Nang said, tightly squeezing both his hands, "you must be very careful on the Ajanti Journey. You can easily die in this song, as you could have in the song where Sardo Numspa trapped you."

"Is this the same song?"

"No. As I have told you, there are many songs. But it is in this song that the Ajanti dagger is kept. You can die here; if you do, our song dies with you. My father

168

knew the danger when he refused my request, but he could not refuse a direct request from the Chosen One. Please be careful."

"Beyond the doors is a path," the Abbot said, pointing to the great set of doors at the end of the room. "Follow it without straying: that is the rule. You may take anything you find beyond those doors, but you must not stray from the path if you hope to retrieve the Ajanti dagger."

"That sounds straightforward enough," Chandler said.

"And you must carry this," the Abbot said, suddenly producing a full glass of water from somewhere within the folds of his robe. "Without spilling any."

Chandler took the glass from the Abbot. Kee Nang stepped forward, as if to embrace him, but the Abbot raised an arm, blocking her path. Chandler, carefully holding the brimming glass in front of him, walked toward the doors, which silently swung open for him. As he passed through, they closed behind him, shutting out all light.

Chandler stood perfectly still in the total darkness, and then gradually became aware of a faint glow before him. The glow became stronger, differentiating into a path which appeared to be composed of light-emitting stones stretching off into the darkness.

He stepped off into the darkness, being careful to stay on the stone-pools of light. After he had gone a short distance, a bright glow appeared to his left. He glanced in that direction, saw a huge mound of gold coins stacked just beyond his reach. To reach the gold, he would only have to take two, at most three, steps off the path of light . . .

You may take anything you find beyond the doors, but . . .

But.

"You've got to be kidding me," Chandler said, and his voice echoed back to him through time and space which he now realized must be cavernous, stretching away on all sides of him, perhaps forever . . .

And to guide him through the eternity of this dimension, he had only the stone-pools of light, which seemed to be getting smaller as he went on . . .

"The path narrows," he mumbled. "I love this shit."

He stepped on a stone-pool which crumbled at the edges. A piece of light snapped off and winked out as it fell into the darkness. Chandler felt a frigid draft puff up around his ankles, and he swayed precariously on the edge of the stone-pool, holding the glass of water tightly with one hand and covering it with the other so as not to spill any.

He did not hear the shard of light land, and he wondered if it would fall forever. As he would fall forever if he slipped . . .

He went on, concentrating on each step so as not to slip or lose his balance. The path continued to narrow, until he finally saw what appeared to be a bamboo suspension bridge about fifty or sixty yards farther on.

He was ten yards from the bridge when he suddenly heard a child crying somewhere in the darkness off to his left. The sound of a child crying had always torn at Chandler's heart, and now he stopped dead in his tracks, balanced on his toes and dangerously spread-eagled between two stone-pools. Once again covering the top of the glass with his hand, he turned his head, saw a little girl of two or three sitting near the edge of a precipice a few feet away, beyond his reach. In her distress the girl was inching closer and closer to the edge of forever . . .

"Don't cry, sweetheart," Chandler said, and immediately felt foolish. He was certain the crying child was just another temptation, like the gold, meant to distract him and take him off the path of light.

The little girl, reacting to the sound of Chandler's voice, abruptly stopped crying. She reached her arms out to him and began to burble happily.

A trick. *Damn* them! Whoever, whatever, "them" is or are. That Sings? It isn't fair.

Chandler sucked in a deep breath, turned away from the child and stepped to the next stone-pool of light. The little girl began to cry again, hysterically, as she saw Chandler apparently abandoning her. Sweat broke out on Chandler's body, and he quickly pirouetted on the narrow stone-pool on which he was standing. His heart was breaking as he watched the child, now kneeling on the very edge of the precipice, reach out over forever . . . for him.

All the world will die . . .

Each time a child dies, Chandler thought, a piece of the world dies anyway. The child might well be an illusion; then again, it might not.

What do you know of these things, Chandler Jarrell? You can take anything you want . . .

He would take this little girl, Chandler thought; if the girl fell to her death, he would die. He had dedicated his life to finding lost children, and this child was nothing if not lost. To abandon this one, regardless of the circumstances, would be to kill the best part of himself.

He would find another way to rescue the Golden Child, Chandler thought. Right now a little girl teetering on the brink of a precipice needed rescuing . . . even if it meant he must leap to the ledge, leaving the path of light and spilling the water.

"It's all right, kid," Chandler said reassuringly. "I'm coming over to get you. Don't move."

The little girl stopped crying, then began to gurgle and laugh as she reached out to him. Chandler crouched, preparing to leap across the void to the ledge . . .

Just as he was about to leap, a woman emerged from the darkness behind the child, scooped up the little girl in her arms. As the woman walked back into the darkness with the laughing child, the little girl waved to Chandler.

And the bamboo bridge Chandler would have been on if he had not stopped for the girl burst into flame.

"The point seems to be that you have to know when to break the rules," Chandler said dryly as he walked forward on a new, broad path of light which led him safely to the ledge where the little girl had been sitting. Here he found the Ajanti dagger, floating in a shimmering pool of deep purple light.

The carving of the Ajanti dagger on his forearm had prepared Chandler for its color and strange, four-bladed appearance—but not for its feel. Chandler almost dropped it into the abyss when he first picked it up. The handle and blades of the dagger neither looked nor felt like steel; the weapon was covered with a green, slimy, lumpy membrane, like the skin of a toad; the thick handle was breathing, like something alive. Fighting off his revulsion, Chandler firmly gripped the slimy, pulsating handle of the dagger with his right hand. Holding the glass of water in his left hand, he turned to go back the way he had come.

The path of light had vanished; there was only the shimmering pool of purple light in which he stood, and he was sinking . . .

To his astonishment, Kee Nang suddenly appeared, swinging down toward him by means of a rope tied to her wrist and anchored somewhere above them in the eternal night. She landed lightly in the pool of purple light.

"Chandler!" Kee Nang cried happily. "You've done it! You have the Ajanti dagger! Give it to me!"

Chandler started to lay the dagger into Kee Nang's outstretched hand, hesitated, then quickly drew it back.

Something was not right.

"Chandler?" Kee Nang continued. "What's wrong? Give me the dagger!"

"I'm the Chosen One," Chandler replied, half turning as if to protect the repulsive, living weapon with his body. "I'll take it back myself."

Kee Nang, the rope still tied around her wrist, stepped closer, thrust out her other hand. "Give me the dagger, you fool!"

This was not Kee Nang, Chandler thought; the eyes of this figure were black but lifeless, lacking the bright gleam of vitality, warmth and intelligence that always shone from Kee Nang's eyes.

Suddenly, he was afraid.

With startling speed and strength, the figure grabbed his forearm and twisted him around, tearing the dagger from his grasp.

Frozen with terror, gutted by despair at the thought that he would fail at what he had thought was his moment of triumph, Chandler could only stand and watch in horror as the figure brought the dagger stabbing down through the air, on a direct line with his heart.

The dagger struck him—but did not penetrate his flesh. Chandler felt as if he had been punched—but not stabbed—in the heart as the dagger struck the piece of tin slung around his neck, creating an explosion of sparks and green flame.

And then the apparition was gone, leaving only the breathing Ajanti dagger lying in the pool of purple light at his feet.

"Shit!" Chandler yelled, and his heart pounded wildly as he bent down and picked up the dagger. He looked at the glass of water in his left hand. Despite the attack by the apparition, he had somehow managed to keep the glass upright, and no water had been spilled. He had his full glass of water, and the Ajanti dagger— but no way of getting back. He was totally surrounded by a void, and he was sinking even deeper into the pool of purple light . . .

Chandler desperately looked around him for some means of escape, but could see none; the darkness was closing in.

And then he saw the rope swinging back toward him. He wondered if the rope itself was an apparition, wondered if he would fall into the abyss if he leaped for it.

But he was going to end up in the abyss anyway if he remained where he was.

His hands weren't free, so he stuck the dagger in his

waistband, wincing as he felt the slimy flesh on the handle breathing against his own flesh, and checked to make certain it was firmly in place. There was still the problem of the water.

The end of the rope was almost upon him. He had to decide.

Without spilling any.

Chandler gulped down the water, flung the empty glass away from him, then leaped from the edge of the pool of purple light and grasped the end of the rope as it swung past him. He swung away into the darkness, which was suddenly warm and comforting.

Chandler blinked and opened his eyes. He was back with Kee Nang and the Abbot of Karma Tang on the elevated vestibule above the great hall, in exactly the same spot where he had been standing when the Abbot had touched his forehead. Below and to his right, the two hundred monks were still there—but now they were standing, facing in his direction, bowing to him. Kee Nang and the Abbot, with Chandler's sheepskin coat draped over his shoulders, were staring at him anxiously.

Everything—almost—was as it had been.

In his right hand he was holding an object with a pulsating, membrane-covered handle that felt like the skin of a toad. The hall was filled with a low murmur which seemed to Chandler to express surprise—and respect.

"You have survived," the Abbot said, making no effort to try to mask his own surprise.

"Thanks to the medallion you gave me," Chandler said quietly, touching the piece of tin hanging around his neck. When he looked down at it, he could see a dent in the center of the metal that had not originally been there. "It saved my life."

The Abbot of Karma Tang shook his head. "It was your life that saved your life. I told you that the fact you couldn't remove the medallion meant that you were made of exceptionally strong, high-quality material. Had I given that medallion to virtually any other man, he would have been able to tear it off and throw it away without any great difficulty. You are truly the Chosen One—and with good reason."

"Welcome back, Chandler," Kee Nang said softly.

Chandler hefted the repulsive, living dagger in his hand, shrugged slightly. "I guess it's time to go back," he said, looking at Kee Nang.

"Chandler," the Abbot said not unkindly, "the terrible weapon you hold can kill the *Gompen Tarma.*"

"I understand, sir."

"And now you dare bargain for the child's life with a creature from the lowest dimension of existence, offering up the one thing the creature wants, because it can kill the child." It was not a question.

"Yes, sir," Chandler said, remembering his own doubts—which remained—and suppressing them. "I don't see that I have any choice."

"It is true, Father," Kee Nang said quickly.

The Abbot bowed slightly, and it seemed to Chandler that the low, constant chanting of the monks in the great hall grew slightly louder, although he knew it could be his imagination.

"You have survived the Ajanti Journey, Chandler

Jarrell, and brought the sacred dagger back to this song. You have earned the right to make these decisions. Our song is in your hands. It is your own, lonely way you must follow."

Chandler swallowed hard. "Sir, may I ask a question? It may seem silly, but—"

"It will not seem silly, Chandler Jarrell," the Abbot of Karma Tang said evenly. "What is it you want to know?"

"This . . . dagger. It's almost a foot long, and just a bit strange—to say the least. It would certainly qualify as a Tibetan antiquity. It would be a tragedy to come all this way for it, and then have it seized by some customs official, or at airport security. I don't know what it's made of, but it certainly feels like steel when you strike with it; I'm afraid it will set off a metal detector at the airport. At the very least, even if they don't take it away from me as a suspected national treasure, I could waste a lot of time trying to explain what it is—at which time they'll certainly lock me up. Finally, if somebody touches this thing, they won't know whether to put it in a box or a cage. I thought maybe a letter or something from you, just in case . . . ?"

"Don't worry, Chandler," the Abbot of Karma Tang said with a warm, somewhat bemused, smile. "Nobody at the airport will question you about the Ajanti dagger."

"Sir, I don't know how much traveling you do, so you may not understand. At the airport they sometimes search luggage, and then there are machines that can detect metal."

"Chandler, it is you who does not understand. How

can something be detected which does not even exist in this dimension?"

"Oh," Chandler said, looking down at the grotesque, green, four-bladed breathing thing in his hand. "You know, sir," he continued, scratching his head, "I'm really sorry I asked."

Chapter Seventeen

FEELING LIKE NOTHING SO MUCH AS A LOVESICK TEENAG-
er, Chandler, hands thrust into his pockets and head
bowed slightly, walked up the gently sloping hillside toward Kee Nang. She was dressed in ceremonial robes
which billowed in the gentle morning breeze, and stood
beneath a tree bursting with yellow fruit. Off to his
right, the temple of Karma Tang gleamed in the
sunlight.

"Uh, hi," Chandler said tentatively.

"Hello, Chandler."

"Nice morning."

"Yes."

There was a prolonged silence, during which an
embarrassed and uncomfortable Chandler felt the
blood rushing to his face. "Loquats," Kee Nang mur-

mured. "We have loquat trees near the house where I grew up." Kee Nang reached up and plucked one of the yellow fruits from the tree. She bit into it, chewed slowly and swallowed. She closed her eyes, and her face was wreathed with a smile.

"Life is sweet."

Chandler plucked a piece of fruit from a limb over his head, bit into it. Instantly, his face contorted; he grimaced, spat out the pulp.

"It's sour!"

"Of course," Kee Nang said, raising one eyebrow slightly. "They're not ripe yet."

Not wanting to disturb the Abbot, who appeared to be in a state of deep meditation, Chandler sat down on the hillside just above the seated, stiff-backed man and waited. An hour went by, and then another, and still the Abbot did not move. Very conscious of the fact that soon they would have to begin their return journey, Chandler finally rose, walked down the hillside, and sat down next to the Abbot. He made a halfhearted attempt to twist his legs into the lotus position, gave up when he felt the familiar cramps begin to knot his thighs.

"Uh . . . excuse me, sir. I'm sorry to disturb you, but I'd very much like to talk to you."

"I know," the Abbot replied evenly. "What took you so long? Do you think I have all day?"

"What?"

"What is it you want, Chandler Jarrell?"

"Advice. You are old and wise. I need to know what words I can use to say to a woman from your world to make her understand that I love her and want to marry her."

180

"You are wasting your time, and mine."

"There are no words?"

The question was met by silence. Chandler waited. There was something about the Abbot's silence that was different, not a rejection. The Abbot seemed to be waiting for him to say something else.

"Actions, sir?" Chandler breathed.

"Ah. Now we are getting somewhere. It is the heart that must speak, and the heart never speaks in words."

"Okay, so what can I do to make her want to marry me?"

The Abbot shrugged. "You sound like a young man in a hurry."

"I am in a hurry."

"But if you took the short path to reach enlightenment, who would want you for a husband? Certainly not a woman from 'my world,' as you put it." The Abbot paused, seemed to ponder something, shrugged. "Then again, enlightenment is enlightenment."

"What's the short path?"

"It is the fastest way to fulfill your destiny. But one slip would mean madness and death."

"This woman is worth the risk. How do I do it?"

"You must keep your priorities straight, to begin with. You are the Chosen One, and our song depends upon your decisions and actions. Consequently, enlightenment on the short path requires that you remain pure until you have done what you must do."

"Pure?" Chandler glanced warily at the old man sitting beside him. "Uh . . . what do you mean by 'pure'?"

The Abbot of Karma Tang snorted with disgust. "You know what I mean; you must accomplish your

181

task before you indulge in physical pleasures."

"That's what I was afraid you meant," Chandler said with a weary sigh. "Is there a long path?"

"Certainly. It takes ten thousand lifetimes."

"I haven't got that kind of time. So no women. What else?"

"No men."

Chandler again glanced into the impassive face of the man next to him to see if the Abbot might be joking. He wasn't.

"That won't be a problem, sir. What else?"

"For you? For the Chosen One, there are three requirements. You must trust someone you have no reason to trust; you must make a promise to someone you have just met; and you must love someone who loves you."

"Oh. Is that all?"

If the Abbot detected the sarcasm in Chandler's voice, his own voice did not reflect it. "That is a great deal."

"Do I have to do those things in that order?"

"No. The decisions about when and how—or whether—to do these things are yours."

"How about if I just walk on water?"

"What would that accomplish?" the Abbot asked in an even tone with no trace of irony.

Chandler sighed. "There's nothing else you can tell me?"

"I tell you that you must tell no one—*no one*—that I have set you on this path. Once again, it is your own lonely way you must go."

Chandler nodded resignedly, rose to his feet. "Thank you for your help, sir."

"You continue to play the fool, Chandler Jarrell. I have not helped you. All I have done is given you an additional burden."

"Father," Kee Nang said quietly, bowing her head, "I have ruined myself for the American. I think I am in love with him."

The Abbot of Karma Tang put his long, tapered fingers beneath his daughter's chin, gently lifted it and smiled into her eyes. "I know you are in love with him."

"He is a fool!" Kee Nang snapped, black eyes flashing.

"Yes," the Abbot replied evenly. "But he is brave."

"He is irresponsible!"

"But he is generous."

"He thinks of nothing but protecting his own feelings!"

"But if you touch his heart, there is nothing he would not do for you."

"He believes in nothing!"

"Ah—but still he does what is right."

"He is a careless, thoughtless, egotistical, undisciplined fool!"

"Yes," the Abbot said, and laughed as he gently squeezed his daughter's shoulders. "I, too, like him very much. It is hard not to." He paused, rubbed his head. "Oh, these magnificent Americans—so much power, and so little understanding of what to do with it."

Kee Nang lowered her gaze, and her voice was barely a whisper. "What should I do?"

"Help him save the *Gompen Tarma*," the Abbot

183

replied without hesitation. "And follow your heart."

Kee Nang nodded, clasped one of the Abbot's hands and pressed her lips to it. "Thank you, Father."

"You are welcome, Daughter. When it is right to marry him, you have my blessing."

"Thank you, Father."

Chapter Eighteen

THERE WAS ONLY THE BARE TWIG LEFT, AND NOW THE dimly glowing boy-child removed that from the folds of his robe, put it into his mouth and slowly began to chew. It was so hard not to give up hope, he thought. So hard . . .

The boy was startled when a dead butterfly suddenly dropped onto the floor just outside his cage. Surprised, he cocked his head and stared at the dead insect lying on the rich, thick carpet. Then he reached out and touched it.

The butterfly slowly began to glow with a luminous light, then abruptly sprang back to life and fluttered away.

The boy-child laughed, his sorrow and worry vanished. He had given life.

Another dead butterfly dropped onto the carpet, and the Golden Child also brought this one to life.

This was his destiny, the boy thought—to bring life and happiness. He could not understand why anyone should want to cause hurt and harm . . .

A third dead butterfly dropped—but this one was too far away for him to reach. Frowning, desperately wanting nothing more than to bring the butterfly back to life, the child strained to reach out and touch the insect.

It was too far.

Suddenly a hand reached down, picked up the dead butterfly and started to bring it closer to the cage.

Laughing with joy, the boy-child reached out and gently touched the hand . . .

Cool lips pressed against his cheek. Chandler opened his eyes to find himself staring up into Kee Nang's face. She was bending over him, kneeling next to the couch in which he was slumped, feet propped up on a coffee table. Someone—Kee Nang—had removed his shoes sometime during the night.

"Sorry," Kee Nang said with an impish grin. "I just couldn't resist. You looked so cute and happy just now, in your sleep . . ."

"He's touched someone," Chandler said, taking his feet off the coffee table and sitting up. For a moment he was disoriented, and could not think where he was. Then he remembered being picked up at the airport by men sent by Dr. Hong—a car and driver for them, two cars for eight burly, armed bodyguards. They had been driven to this house in the woods, high up in the Malibu hills. They had arrived after sundown; he had poured

186

himself a drink, sat down on the couch to talk with Kee Nang about what he seemed to perceive as a new warmth toward him, a change of attitude . . . It was the last he remembered.

"Who's touched who, Chandler?"

"Nothing," Chandler said, shaking his head in an effort to chase his continuing drowsiness. In the center of the coffee table in front of him was the briefcase in which he had put the Ajanti dagger. On top of the briefcase was the set of shiny new handcuffs he had insisted they purchase on the way to the house. "God, Kee Nang, I can't understand why I'm so tired."

"You've had a very long journey."

"So have you," Chandler said, resisting the impulse to reach out and stroke the woman's raven hair. Instead he rubbed his knuckles into his eyes. "I shouldn't be suffering any more from jet lag than you."

"I wasn't talking about the flight from Tibet," Kee Nang said with a little laugh. "I meant your journey to obtain the Ajanti dagger. Now *there's* a trip that will give you jet lag."

Chandler smiled at the face he found so beautiful. "I guess you're right. But I can't afford to be tired now. We have to get moving, do . . . whatever it is we have to do now."

He started to rise, was firmly pushed back down on the sofa by Kee Nang's hand on his chest.

"You are not ready, Chandler. You are not rested."

"There's no time to rest, Kee Nang. That son-of-a-bitch Numspa is lying low for some reason, and the child is very close to death. I feel it."

"I understand. But you still remain the *Gompen Tarma*'s only chance for life. You are about to engage in

187

the deadliest duel any man has ever fought, against the deadliest opponent any man has ever faced. You must be as strong as possible. To try to save a few hours now at the risk of losing everything there is would not be a wise expenditure of time, would it?"

"We have to get going, Kee Nang. Just get me a cup of coffee. I'll be all right."

"I think I have something that will work for you better than a cup of coffee," Kee Nang said with a coquettish smile, and stood up.

Chandler was pleased to see that Kee Nang was dressed in a filmy, flesh-colored negligee. Now that she was standing, he could see that her hair fell more fully around her shoulders, framing her face.

She had removed the four jeweled pins.

Kee Nang stepped to one side. Although the first rays of dawn were seeping through the windows in the rest of the house, the first-floor bedroom behind Kee Nang was awash in luminescent gem-glow. She had set the pins in place on the walls.

"All *right*," Chandler said, springing to his feet. And then he remembered. He stopped, moved away from her.

"Chandler? What's wrong?"

"Nothing. I just . . . can't."

"You *can't*?"

"I . . . don't want to, Kee Nang. Not now."

Chandler turned away from the hurt in the woman's eyes, glanced into the bedroom—and started when he saw the dark shadows moving like ghosts in the radiant light. "Something's wrong," he said curtly.

Kee Nang glanced at him, frowned. "What?"

"I . . . don't know."

Kee Nang smiled tentatively. "What could be wrong? This house is safe, Chandler. And even if it weren't, we are protected from evil by bodyguards, two each at the north, south, east and west."

"They're dead—or soon will be."

"What? How do you know?"

"Look in the light."

Kee Nang turned, peered into the bedroom, looked back at him. "It's beautiful; all I see there is our pleasure—or I did before you refused me."

But Chandler saw the alien shapes, like gobs of oil in water, coalesce, dissolve, then reform into new shadows that moved in the gem-glow. The shapes filled him with terror, and he began taking deep breaths in an effort to calm himself. He knew what the shapes meant—they were here, come for him, Kee Nang, and the Ajanti dagger. He had rested too long; there had never been time to rest, and he should have known that. Sardo Numspa hadn't been "lying low"; he'd been stalking . . .

"Chandler . . . ?"

Chandler wheeled around, hurried back to the sofa. He found his shoes beneath the coffee table, slipped them on. Then he cuffed the handle of the briefcase to his left wrist, and slipped the key into the shoe on his right foot. Gripping the briefcase firmly with his left hand, and Kee Nang's elbow with his right, he led her out of the living room and into the kitchen, to the back door.

"Chandler?" Kee Nang continued, partially resisting the insistent pressure on her elbow. "What are you *talking* about? I didn't see anything in the light."

"I did," Chandler replied tersely. His growing terror

was making him feel nauseous and dizzy. "We have to get out of here."

"But where will we go?!"

"Any place that's away from here."

Chandler slowly opened the door, cautiously peered out into the dawn. Suddenly Kee Nang stepped outside and stopped in front of him, standing very close.

"You are right," Kee Nang said in a low, tense voice. "They are here; now I feel it. Come. I will lead us out of here. We will walk directly into the sun; it is the safest route."

Kee Nang, grasping Chandler's hand tightly, led him due east into the rising sun, which appeared as glowing bars of rose-colored light through the tall trees which surrounded the house.

They passed two dead guards. One of the men had a knife buried to the hilt in his chest; the other had a deep gash completely encircling his twisted, broken neck.

The monkey man's whip had killed the second man, Chandler thought, and shuddered. He had made a terrible mistake. There was not going to be any trade; like a fool, he had obtained the Ajanti dagger and now Sardo Numspa and his legions were marching toward him, coming to take the dagger and then destroy him and all that he loved.

Suddenly Kee Nang stopped so quickly that Chandler, looking back over his shoulder for signs of pursuit, almost bumped into her. He reached out to grip her arm, then felt his breath catch in his throat.

Ten feet in front of them, a black mist oozed up from the ground, eclipsing the bars of sunlight shining through the trees behind it. There was a sharp, hissing sound, and an instant later Sardo Numspa—impeccably dressed in his gray suit, cape, and black English riding boots with gold spurs—stepped out of the cloud of fetid gas.

"Good morning sports fans," Sardo Numspa said, and grinned triumphantly.

Chandler shoved Kee Nang to the ground, then screamed with frustration and rage and leaped at Sardo Numspa, raising the briefcase to strike at the figure's head. There was a sharp, metallic crack, and his arm was almost torn out of its socket as the monkey man's whip lashed around the briefcase and then violently yanked backward. Chandler was turned around, then yanked off his feet. He landed painfully on his side, rolled, scrambled to his feet—and froze when he saw the monkey man standing a few feet away next to a tree, an obscene leer fixed on his leathery, simian features as he pulled on the whip-trapped briefcase, pulling Chandler's arm taut.

"Chandler!" Kee Nang screamed from where she lay on the ground. *"Watch out!"*

Chandler yanked back. He dug his heels into the thick loam and moss at his feet and pulled on the briefcase with all his might. He went back a few inches—just far enough so that the sword arcing down through the air from his blind side missed his wrist and smashed through the handcuff chain with a loud click. Chandler tumbled on his back, while the briefcase containing the Ajanti dagger sailed through the air toward the monkey man.

He was lost, Chandler thought as he started to get up, then resignedly sank back down; Sardo Numspa, flanked by the monkey man and a raider holding a sword and a steel crossbow, stood a few feet away, watching him, triumphant expressions on their faces. The monkey man was holding the briefcase to his hairy chest.

The world was lost.

The second raider, reacting to a hand signal from his master, notched an arrow into the crossbow, handed the weapon to Sardo Numspa.

Chandler, his soul writhing in agony, looked over at Kee Nang, who still lay on the ground a few yards away where he had shoved her. "I'm sorry," he said simply.

Sardo Numspa's face was changing now, transmogrifying into that of a slime-coated, fanged rodent with enormous eyes of fire in blood. His forked tongue darted out across the distance between him and Chandler, vibrated in the air less than an inch from Chandler's eyes.

"I want to thank you for being so cooperative in bringing me the Ajanti dagger, Mr. Jarrell," the rodent-faced thing hissed as it slowly brought the crossbow up into firing position. "When I demanded it, it was just a ploy—something designed to distract you and buy time while I tried to figure other ways of destroying the child. I never imagined that the Abbot of Karma Tang would be fool enough to allow you to attempt the Ajanti Journey, or that you would survive if he did. My cup runneth over."

Then Sardo Numspa fired an arrow straight at Chandler's heart.

Kee Nang had jumped to her feet as Sardo Numspa had fired the crossbow, and had leaped in front of Chandler. Now the arrow pierced her chest with a sound that ripped Chandler's heart. Kee Nang half-turned, collapsed in Chandler's arms.

"Oh, no," Chandler moaned, rocking back and forth. "God, no."

"Well, well," Sardo Numspa said as he handed the crossbow back to the raider and took the briefcase from the monkey man. "What have we here?"

"Damn you!" Chandler shrieked in mindless fury. *"Damn you!"*

"Tut-tut, Mr. Jarrell," the creature with the fire-in-blood eyes hissed. "Let's not lose our temper. How lovely that the woman took the arrow meant for you. Now, I believe it would be unfitting for me to put you out of your misery; you have so much to think about, so much grief to live with." The creature's lips pulled back from its fangs in a horrible caricature of a smile. "Have a nice day, Mr. Jarrell."

And then the three figures vanished into the tar-colored mist.

"Oh, Kee Nang," Chandler moaned, cradling the woman in his arms. Blood flowed freely from the wound in her chest, and he could not staunch it.

Kee Nang looked up at him, smiled weakly. Already, a film of death was spreading over the surface of her eyes, dulling their light. She whispered to him. "I didn't sleep with you to obligate you; I slept with you because I love you."

Bitter, hot tears flooded Chandler's eyes, flowed down his cheeks. The grief and regret pressing on him seemed heavy enough to crush his heart, sharp enough to split him in two. "Kee Nang . . . Kee Nang . . ."

Kee Nang opened her mouth to speak again, but could make only a faint, sighing sound. Chandler drew her even closer, bent down so that his ear was next to her mouth.

"Chandler," Kee Nang breathed, her words just barely audible, "you have not lost yet. He made a mistake in letting you live. You must fight on to the end, even if all hope seems lost. You must not allow my death to paralyze your will. Go to Dr. Hong. He will advise you now. Don't give up, Chandler. Fight to the . . ."

Chandler sat for long moments, rocking back and forth as he cradled Kee Nang's lifeless body in his arms. Finally he yanked the arrow from her chest, hurled it away.

All the world . . .

You are the Chosen One . . .

The Ajanti dagger is a double-edged weapon . . .

Don't give up hope . . .

Fight to the end . . .

With tears blurring his vision and dripping from his face into the blood-soaked ground, Chandler lifted Kee Nang's body in his arms and staggered back through the death-stained dawn toward the house.

Chapter Nineteen

THE WONDROUS LIGHT IN HER EYES WAS GONE FROM HER in death, Chandler thought as he vacantly stared down at Kee Nang's body, which had been laid out on a table in the dimly-lit back room of Dr. Hong's herb shop. A curtain had been drawn back from a window high on the wall behind the table, and a single shaft of bright sunlight pierced the gloom and illuminated Kee Nang's still head and shoulders.

He realized now that he had already lost the world when Kee Nang had died; she had become his world.

Have a nice day . . .

"She saved my life," Chandler groaned, arching his head back and clenching his jaws. His grief was like a razor shredding his entrails, making the air in his lungs feel like broken glass.

"Now you must save hers," came the dry, rasping

voice of Kala, who still sat half-naked behind her candle-lit scrim. "Stop sniveling."

"She's dead!" Chandler snarled back at the shadow-figure.

"The *Gompen Tarma* can bring he¬ back to life. As long as sunlight still shines on her body, the touch of the *Gompen Tarma* will heal her wound and restore life to her."

Chandler swallowed hard, found that his mouth was bone-dry. His tongue felt thick, filling the back of his throat. "Sardo Numspa took the Ajanti dagger. The child is dead by now."

"The *Gompen Tarma* is not dead yet, fool! I would know if the child was dead! *Fool!* You are wasting time! Instead of standing here weeping, you should be searching for the child!"

Chandler's grief was suddenly supplanted by rage, and he clenched his fists and glared at the silhouette on the silken scrim. *"How?! Where?!"*

"You are the Chosen One, fool! You must find the child! Go, now! You have already wasted too much precious time! You have only a few hours of daylight left!"

"Damn you, bitch!" Chandler shouted, his words festering with hate and fury. "I never asked to be any goddam Chosen One, and it was you people who convinced me I had to play Sardo Numspa's game and get the dagger! Now, as for you, bitch—!"

Trembling with an explosive mixture of grief and fury, Chandler grabbed the material of the scrim with both hands, yanked it to the floor—and then jumped back, his heart pounding wildly in his chest. He opened his mouth to scream, but no sound would come out.

Kala, possessor of the beautiful face and breasts,

hissed with rage as she quickly rearranged her human torso on the heavy, scaled coils of her lower body. The huge rattles on the end of her tail rustled ominously, and then she slowly rose into the air on her snake coils. She stretched out her arms and hovered over Chandler, her head and torso now resembling nothing so much as the hood of a cobra. Kala's full, sensuous lips parted slightly, and a tiny, pink, forked tongue flicked out. The hiss that was her voice now not only rasped in Chandler's ears, but scraped in his mind as he turned and blindly fled, caroming off the walls of the dark, narrow corridor outside the room, smashing into the painting of Sardo Numspa . . .

"Bring the Child!"

Chapter Twenty

IT WAS HOPELESS, CHANDLER THOUGHT AS HE DROVE aimlessly through the bronze-colored late afternoon. Where could he look? Anywhere—and nowhere; one place was as good as another. He had no clue whatsoever to where the child had been taken or why Sardo Numspa hadn't killed him yet. He did have the dagger, after all.

The little boy was probably already dead.

I would know . . .

But would *he* know? Chandler wondered. Would the world end in a bang or a whimper? Would this song flash away in an instant, or slowly evaporate over a thousand years?

His world was already dead.

Finally he drove out of the city limits, up Mulholland Drive. High above the city, he pulled over to the side of the road, turned off the engine, and slumped over the wheel. The sun was going down.

Don't give up hope . . .

"You were my hope," Chandler said aloud.

And then he heard the unmistakable, clear trill of the rainbow-bird. Behind him. Chandler twisted around in his seat, and his heart began to pound when he saw the bird with the brilliant plumage hovering in the air over the road, twenty yards away. The bird flew away a short distance, then darted back to its original position and hovered. Its song was achingly beautiful and sweet . . . and urgent.

The bird was waiting for him, calling him.

Chandler started the engine. He slammed the gears into reverse, spun the car around, then shifted and raced after the rainbow-bird, which was now flying straight ahead, only a few feet above the ground and just in front of the car's hood.

Suddenly the bird banked and darted to its left. Chandler slammed on the brakes, spun the wheel, and took the turn onto a narrow, rutted dirt road on two wheels. He straightened the fishtailing car and raced after the bird. He had gone only a few hundred yards when he saw, on his right, a stone wall. The bird once again banked sharply, then disappeared into the trees on the other side of the wall.

Chandler brought the car to a skidding halt in the middle of the road, pushed open the door and leaped out. He glanced quickly to the west, where the sun continued to inexorably sink toward the horizon, then took five quick running steps and leaped up the wall. His fingers caught the top and, with strength born of desperation, he pulled himself up—but not over. He crouched on the foot-wide ledge that was the top of the wall, heart hammering, uncertain what to do next.

Below him, stretching in all directions as far as he could see, the ground was covered by a thick bed of what looked like ivy—except that it was flecked with bubbling, blood-colored foam. From somewhere deep within the bleeding ivy there came an ominous, hissing rumble that made the flecked leaves tremble and throw off specks of red foam.

Chandler leaped out into space and caught hold of a low-hanging limb of a tree. He swung once, then used the momentum of his second swing to carry him up onto another, nearby limb. There he paused to catch his breath and look around him. From his perch he could see through, and beyond, the grove of trees. He had perhaps twenty-five more yards of bleeding ivy to cross, which he was fairly certain he could do by climbing through the trees. Beyond the trees and ivy was a lawn, a concrete patio—and a door in the side of an enormous, looming gray mansion.

He had to hurry, Chandler thought; he estimated that he had perhaps an hour and a half of sunlight left—at most. He not only had to find and rescue the child from somewhere within the enormous mansion, but then escape and make it back to Los Angeles, to Chinatown, before night settled in.

He heard an ominous whistling sound, and reflexively ducked a fraction of a second before the monkey man's multi-sectioned steel whip cracked in the air an inch above his head. He turned, felt his heart contract in terror when he saw the monkey man squatting on the limb of a neighboring tree, only a few feet away. Now the terrible smell of the creature came to Chandler.

The monkey man's simian features drew back in an evil grin; his hand came up, the whip lashed out . . .

Chandler sprang to the branch above his head, swung up on it as the whip cracked inches below his feet. He scrambled along the limb to the trunk, paused there for a moment, then leaped to a still higher branch in another tree. Fighting to stave off panic, trembling with fear—for himself, the Golden Child, the world—he looked around him, saw nothing.

Suddenly he smelled something. He turned around, looked down—saw the monkey man crouched on a limb a few feet below him. The grin on the creature's face was now even broader.

It was useless to attempt to escape this way, Chandler thought. He was being toyed with; he could not hope to outpace, or hide from, the monkey man in the creature's own element. He had absolutely no time to waste—and with that thought he flung himself headfirst through the air. He hit the thoroughly startled monkey man squarely in the center of the chest. Both of them toppled off the limb on which the monkey man had been squatting, and plummeted toward the bleeding, trembling ivy bed below. In blind desperation, Chandler reached out—and felt the palm of his right hand slap against the rough bark of a tree limb. His fingers locked around the tree limb, and he was whipped around in the air. He hung, swinging, precipitously, by one hand, then managed to get his other hand on the limb and pull himself up as he heard the monkey man begin to scream in a high-pitched, keening, animal squeal. The squealing was quickly drowned out by even more terrible crunching sounds that seemed to come from everywhere in the ivy below him.

Chandler looked down and moaned with horror as he

watched the monkey man, as if trapped in hungry quicksand—horribly spurting blood from his mouth, ears and nostrils—slowly sink beneath the surface of the bleeding ivy, which was now churning and frothing.

Chandler shook his head to try to clear his mind of the horror he had just witnessed—and his terror of slipping—and resumed his clumsy but effective passage through the trees. He jumped and swung from one branch to another like a bizarre Tarzan-in-training, making his way to the edge of the trees. There was a last, open expanse of the frothing, carnivorous ivy perhaps ten feet wide.

Chandler hung from a limb and began to swing back and forth. At the apogee of his most powerful swing, he released his grip and kicked his feet up at the darkening sky. He sailed through the air, landed in a hedge just beyond the deadly ivy bed. He immediately rolled out of the hedge and, keeping low, sprinted across the lawn and the concrete patio. He flattened himself against the mansion, next to the door, and gasped for breath, at the same time listening intently for sounds of alarm. He heard none. His presence had not been detected—yet.

So little time—not even enough to catch his breath.

He tried the door; it opened. He slipped into the mansion, immediately crouched down behind a chair near the door in what appeared to be a large, richly decorated sitting room. When he still heard nothing, he slowly raised himself up and barely managed to choke off a cry of hope and joy; at the far side of the room, the faintly throbbing Ajanti dagger rested on a black felt pad in a glass case set on top of a marble pedestal.

There was no one else in the room.

He darted out from behind the chair and across the room to the pedestal. He raised the hinged top of the glass case and lifted out the green-skinned Ajanti dagger.

He felt, rather than heard, a presence in the doorway behind him, and he spun around, the Ajanti dagger thrust out in front of him to defend, to kill. Til, the giant with the thick callus on his forehead, stood unmoving, hands at his sides, gazing calmly at Chandler. Even with the deadly, otherworldly dagger only inches from his heart, Til did not seem to be afraid. He appeared to be waiting for something, his death, perhaps, or . . .

Stab! Chandler thought. A quick thrust, and he would have one less enemy to worry about.

But Chandler did not move. Something in the giant's eyes held him transfixed. Til had changed, Chandler thought. Or been changed. Profoundly. Now Chandler thought he saw compassion and kindness in the other man's face and eyes.

Maybe. The giant could simply be waiting for the dagger to move away from his chest before he attacked with the battering ram of his head.

The Golden Child had touched someone. Til?

Decide!

If he was wrong, if he decided to trust this fearsome member of the raiding party and ended with his skull bashed in, there would be no joy or hope left for anyone.

The giant very slowly brought his hands up to his chest, clasped them together in a prayerful gesture, then nodded toward the corridor behind him. Chandler hesitated—then abruptly lowered the dagger. Immediately, Til motioned for Chandler to follow him. Then, moving with surprising speed and agility for such a big man, he led Chandler out of the sitting room and down the corridor, through another room with sheet-draped furniture, and down another corridor, moving ever farther into the depths of the mansion. Then, finally, he came to an abrupt stop outside a large, bronze-plated door, and motioned for Chandler to remain in the corridor while he went into the room. Chandler was reluctant to let the giant out of his sight, but decided that he no longer had any real choice but to trust Til completely. He nodded. The giant nodded back, then opened the door and stepped into the room.

Chandler waited. Then, suddenly, the raider with the crossbow stepped out of the room and into the corridor. He saw Chandler, raised the weapon . . .

Before the raider could pull the trigger on the crossbow, Til came hurtling out of the room. He knocked the crossbow from the raider's hands, grasped the man by his upper arms, then brought his callused forehead crashing down onto the top of the other man's head. There was a cracking sound, like pottery being broken; Til released his grip on the man's arms, and the dead raider crumpled to the floor.

Now Til motioned for Chandler to enter the room. Chandler did so, but stopped just inside the doorway as tears of joy welled in his eyes and rolled down his cheeks. He groped behind him until he found the giant's hand, squeezed it.

A naked chanter hung, crucified, on each of the four walls of the room. In the center of the room, sitting in the twelve-armed cage, was the Golden Child.

Chapter Twenty-One

CHANDLER WAS HALFWAY TO THE CAGE WHEN THE CRUCI-fied chanter on the wall to his right exploded in a ball of black flame. The flame instantly spread across the wall, dissolving it. Beyond the black flame, from somewhere across space and time, Chandler heard a chorus of agonized screams which seemed to resonate with the howling of his own soul as Sardo Numspa—his gray suit, cape and boots untouched by the flame—stepped out of the holocaust.

First the creature's eyes turned to pupils of fire in pools of blood . . . and then the rest of it began to change as smoke rose from the clothing, which began to fall away.

Chandler ran to the cage, snapped open the arms and lifted the child, cradling him in the crook of his left arm. Then, shielding the little boy with his body and holding the Ajanti dagger out in front of him, he slowly backed toward the door. Chandler watched in horrified fascination as two black, leathery, clawed wings suddenly unfolded from Sardo Numspa's back and stretched up over its head, virtually filling half the room. The wings kept expanding until their tips touched opposite walls, smashing the lights.

Now, at last, the beast that was Sardo Numspa was revealed in its true form—a shape which he had seen in a painting, and which had burned in his mind since then.

Chandler did not even realize that, frozen with awe and terror, he had stopped moving until the giant brushed him aside, bounded across the room and leaped at the head of the beast. Til wrapped his thick arms tightly around the long, writhing neck of the creature and began to butt with his callused forehead against Sardo Numspa's foaming, fanged maw. Again and again Til banged, unfeeling, oblivious. The creature shrieked as one, long fang was broken off—and then skewered the giant with the remaining three.

Chandler wheeled and ran out of the room, slamming the door shut behind him.

Holding the child to his breast, moving with a speed he had not known he possessed, Chandler ran back the way he had come. Behind him, in pursuit, something of awesome size and strength was smashing through walls in its passage . . .

Somewhere he had made a wrong turn which brought him to the right place—the front of the house. He ran out the open door, bounded down marble steps, then slid to a halt on the loose gravel of the driveway when he saw two cars and the white van parked to the side, facing the road. The keys were in the ignition of the first car, a red Pontiac Firebird. Chandler opened the door, leaned in and placed the little boy in the bucket seat on the passenger's side, then slid in behind the wheel. When he glanced at the boy, he was astonished to find the child smiling at him—confident, apparently totally unafraid.

"I'm glad to see you're having such a good time, kid," Chandler said through clenched jaws as he turned the key in the ignition. The engine whined and sputtered, but did not turn over. He pumped the accelerator once, and turned the key again—with the same result. "It's all right, kid. I'm going to get you out of here, and that's a promise."

"I know you will, Chandler," the little boy said in a little boy's voice as he reached across the space between the bucket seats and touched the dagger-scar on Chandler's right forearm. "Thank you for not giving up. I love you."

"Right," Chandler grunted, stunned by how the boy's simple, gentle touch had chased the terror from his heart, and replaced it with renewed courage. He had stopped trembling. "Fasten your seat belt, kiddo, because this is going to be a rough ride—if we ever get started."

Behind them, the mansion was crumbling in a wave of booming sounds, sending up clouds of dust, as Sardo Numspa crashed through its bowels, coming after them . . .

Out of the corner of his eye, Chandler saw the ends of the little boy's seat belt—without being touched—rise into the air, wrap around the boy, and snap shut. A moment later, Chandler's seat belt did the same.

"I love it," Chandler said as he turned the key in the ignition a third time and the engine roared to life.

Chandler put the car into gear and stamped on the accelerator. The Firebird shot out of the driveway, leaving in its wake a plume of flying gravel, at the same time as the last of the mansion behind them collapsed and something dark passed overhead, eclipsing what little sunlight was left. A blast of foul-smelling wind hit them, rocking the car; Chandler shuddered as a wave of intense cold passed through him. At the end of the driveway he whipped the wheel to the left and shot down the dirt road back toward Mulholland, swerving up on a shoulder in order to avoid hitting his own car. He reached Mulholland, turned right, then again put the accelerator to the floor. Below them, to their left, was the city of Los Angeles: the red-orange ball of the sun was continuing to sink toward the horizon, and people had already begun to turn on their lights.

Chandler glanced in the rearview mirror, and felt his stomach muscles tighten when he saw a black stain moving across the sky, soaring high in the distance. Chandler looked back toward the road, swerved to avoid a large pothole. When he again looked in the rearview mirror, he was startled to see that, in only a second or two, the stain that was Sardo Numspa had grown to such size that it cast a shadow over the entire length of a bridge over a deep gulley to their left, part of an alternate route into the city.

The stain was closing on them . . .

Suddenly the dark, winged shape swooped down and clipped a high-voltage power line just behind them, and Chandler's vision in the rearview mirror was obscured by sparks and smoke as the line fell across the road. The enormous shape passed by overhead, and Chandler barely had time to brake the car to a skidding, shuddering halt. A second power line had fallen across the road in front of them where it lay sparking, jumping and twitching like some electrocuted living thing in torment.

Then the shadow that was Sardo Numspa lifted. Chandler tensed, listening and watching—and in a few moments the darkness and intense cold returned, accompanied by the sound of tearing metal just above his head. Chandler unbuckled the child's seat belt and clasped the boy to his breast an instant before an enormous, black claw crashed through the roof of the car and stabbed and groped in the space where the child had been sitting.

Then the windshield shattered, showering powdered glass over the car's interior.

The thing would have the car torn apart in another few seconds, Chandler thought as he slipped back through the space between the bucket seats into the rear seat, and he seemed to have no choice now but to try to somehow escape in the open. He kicked open the left rear door and jumped out. Hunched over the child in his arms, he ducked under the swipe of a clawed wing and raced down the side of the gulley, the blood-red glow of the setting sun in his eyes. He heard a whooshing sound behind him and fell to the ground, shielding the boy with his body, as the black, gelid shape passed by just inches overhead. Then Chandler glanced at the boy; the Golden Child, his head pressed against Chandler's chest, seemed perfectly serene.

Chandler wondered if the little boy was really as unafraid as he appeared, or was simply resigned to death.

He was not resigned to death; the child must not die.

211

Chandler jumped to his feet, desperately looking around him for some kind of shelter. Off to his right he saw a narrow, dark aperture in the side of one of the enormous, concrete pillars supporting the bridge over the gulley. He sprinted across the hillside, reached the narrow opening and slipped through into semi-darkness just as the even greater darkness on wings swooped past. There was the sound of claws scraping on concrete, rising . . .

There was no way that Sardo Numspa in his true form was going to squeeze through the aperture, Chandler thought—which meant that they might be safe, at least for a few minutes. But a few more minutes was all he had.

The child can bring her back to life . . .

So little time to save Kee Nang from eternal night; a half hour, perhaps just a bit more . . .

But how?!

Don't give up hope . . .

Keep going.

Chandler shoved the Ajanti dagger into his waistband; then, holding the child under his left arm, he began struggling up a ladder comprised of steel rungs embedded in one wall of the hollow concrete pillar. Halfway up, the muscles in his arms and back began to burn with fatigue from the exertion of climbing with one hand. He paused to gasp for air.

Keep going!

He reached the top, stepped off the last rung onto a two-yard-wide concrete catwalk that was just beneath the roadway, and appeared to run the length of the bridge. He set down the child, then pushed with all his might against a manhole grate just above his head. The steel cover didn't budge. Chandler sucked in a deep breath, gritted his teeth, and shoved again; there was still no movement.

There was a sound like a clap of thunder, and the entire structure shook as the creature that was Sardo Numspa came crashing down through the roadway. Slime sprayed through the air, and Chandler once again shielded the boy with his body as shards of concrete and steel showered down on the catwalk and into the yawning, black space beneath them.

Something was clawing at his ankle, grabbing, pulling him backward toward the lip of the ledge . . .

Chandler snatched the Ajanti dagger from his waistband, twisted around and stabbed into the darkness at the clawing thing on his ankle. There was a deafening screech that echoed through the concrete chamber, bringing down even more debris from the broken roadway above. Chandler looked up at the sky through the hole in the roadway at the dust swirling in the rays of the setting sun . . .

A large chunk of concrete flew through the air just above his head and smashed into a concrete support wall just behind him. Another flew past, missed, fell away into the darkness. Chandler spun around—just in time to see a third hunk of stone flying directly toward his head. There was no time to duck, and Chandler reflexively threw up his hands in a feeble gesture to protect himself as best he could.

The hunk of concrete veered away at a sharp angle at the last moment and sailed up through the hole in the roadway. Chandler looked around in amazement.

The Golden Child was standing in a shaft of red, dust-speckled sunlight which fell through the hole in the roadway; the muscles in the child's face were clenched like a fist as he summoned all his remaining strength to protect Chandler.

Another concrete chunk came hurtling at him from out of the darkness to his left, veered upward and sailed through the hole.

The little boy was very weak, Chandler thought, and his concentration couldn't last much longer. He took the Ajanti dagger in his right hand, turned to his left, crouched in the rubble on the catwalk, and waited . . .

What emerged from the darkness was Sardo Numspa as a gentleman—but now one trouser leg of his gray suit hung in tatters, and green slime flowed from a gaping wound in his right leg, dripped away in flashes of luminescent green fire. Pale green fire crackled around the creature as it tore loose a huge chunk of concrete from the roof; then, dragging its mangled leg behind it, Sardo Numspa lurched forward, raised the boulder into the air to bring it crashing down on Chandler's head . . .

Chandler reared back, flung the Ajanti dagger.

The four-bladed, living dagger passed through the bubble of fire around the creature with a sound like a rifle shot, and buried itself to the hilt in Sardo Numspa's chest. Screeching, its hands clutched around the dagger embedded in its chest, the fire-eyed creature toppled off the catwalk and fell into the darkness. There was a roar as a great section of the roadway collapsed and fell after Sardo Numspa, burying him in tons of rubble.

Now the whole bridge began to shudder and sway. Chandler swept the child up in his arms and scrambled up the side of a huge mound of rubble, through the hole in the roadway and onto the wildly swaying bridge.

Holding the child to his breast with both hands, he sprinted back toward where the Firebird was parked, a hundred yards away. As he reached the car, the entire bridge collapsed with a prolonged, rumbling roar.

He got into the car, carefully placed the child on the glass-crusted seat next to him, and turned on the engine. He drove carefully up on the shoulder of the road to bypass the fallen power line, which was still sparking, came back down on the road and floored the accelerator.

Careening down Mulholland Drive, Chandler drove in a kind of trance where time was suspended. He was oblivious of all else but the one thing he knew he must do. Driving at speeds which occasionally passed a hundred miles an hour, weaving through traffic, running lights, he had the sensation that he was alone, looking down a long, dark tunnel toward the silhouette of a woman who was reaching out for him . . .

Kee Nang would be there at the end of the tunnel waiting for him, Chandler thought.

If he could get the Golden Child to her before the sun went down.

But the light was growing increasingly dimmer as he raced through the streets of Los Angeles; day and hope were dying.

By the time he reached the herb shop, there was only a blood-red sliver of sun remaining on the little pieces of horizon visible between buildings. He drove the car up on the curb in front of the herb shop, pushed open his door and turned in his seat—but the Golden Child had already gotten out of the car and was entering the shop, as if he knew exactly why Chandler had brought him there, and what was expected of him.

They were going to make it, Chandler thought, his

heart pounding with joy as he ran into the shop and found the Golden Child waiting for him. Kee Nang was going to live . . .

He picked the child up in his arms, ran with him through the curtain at the rear of the shop, down the narrow corridor and through the second curtain over the entrance to the room at the back of the building.

Dr. Hong was sitting on a stool next to the scrim, his hands clasped between his knees. The heads of both the old Chinese and the snake-woman behind the candle-lit scrim were bowed in grief and resignation. Chandler looked at the still figure of Kee Nang lying on the table next to the wall, and cried aloud.

The woman he loved was now almost totally shrouded in darkness—except for a single, tiny bar of light illuminating the toes of her right foot.

Still, it was sunlight.

As long as sunlight shines on her . . .

He was not too late.

Chandler set the boy down, gripped his hand. He started to lead the boy toward the table—then stopped and jumped back as the floor cracked open directly in front of him. Flame and fetid air leaped out of the crack, followed by Sardo Numspa. Oozing a steady flow of green slime from the wound in its human-form leg and the even greater hole in its chest, the creature lurched forward and raised the Ajanti dagger to strike at the Golden Child.

Chandler yanked the little boy behind him as the dagger arced down and struck the medallion on his chest in an explosion of green flame and sparks which lit the room. Chandler was left unharmed. Shrieking with rage, hatred and an inconsolable sense of loss,

216

Chandler savagely ripped the Ajanti dagger from the creature's grasp. He raised the dagger over his head with both hands, went up on his toes, then slammed the dagger to the hilt into one of Sardo Numspa's fire-in-blood eyes.

Sardo Numspa's banshee howl filled the world, like a great, raging tempest of evil. Then his head imploded into nothingness, followed by the rest of him. The beast Sardo Numspa winked out of existence into silence, never again to be heard in earth's song, or any other.

To Chandler, the silence that followed was almost as deafening as the creature's howl—and in that silence, Chandler could hear the weeping of his soul.

To his right, Kala's lifeless, half-human and half-serpent body lay in the folds of the shredded scrim, draped across Dr. Hong's corpse. Chandler sobbed, then staggered to the table, where Kee Nang's body was now completely shrouded in night.

The song of the earth would continue, he thought as he raised the woman by the shoulders and cradled her in his arms, but Kee Nang would not be part of it. The song would continue, but he would hear no music.

He felt a tiny hand touch his elbow, and he glanced down into the smiling face of the little boy. Whatever else he was and could do, Chandler thought, the Golden Child was still . . . a child . . . and he could not be expected to understand the grief Chandler was feeling. Chandler tried to smile back, but his lips trembled, and he could only sob.

The little boy continued to smile as he suddenly gripped Kee Nang's left ankle with both hands and raised it into the air, into the last needle of light radiated by the sun before it finally sank below the horizon.

Immediately, Kee Nang's arms came up and wrapped themselves around Chandler's neck. Then she dropped one hand onto the little boy's head, raised her head and rested it on Chandler's shoulder, gently placed her warm lips on his neck.

Chapter Twenty-Two

CHANDLER CALLED CHERYL MOSELY'S MOTHER FROM THE airport to tell the woman that the men who had killed her daughter were themselves now dead. He hung up the receiver, bought a Dodgers baseball cap in a souvenir shop, then walked back across the marble floor of the main passengers' lounge, where Kee Nang and the Golden Child stood at a huge observation window, watching baggage being loaded aboard planes on the tarmac below.

"They'll be calling you to board soon," Chandler said, wrapping his arms around the woman and child.

"I'll miss you," Kee Nang said, looking at him with her limpid, black eyes.

"Oh, and I'll miss you." Chandler felt a lump growing in his throat. He quickly took the baseball cap out of his pocket and put it on the Golden Child's head.

"Here, kid. You'll need this. It's *very* cold in Tibet; I know."

The little boy looked up, grinning, and put his hand in Chandler's.

"I wasn't around a thousand years ago," Kee Nang said, hugging Chandler's waist, "or a thousand years before that, to see how things were done, but, as Chosen Ones go, you've got to be the best."

Chandler laughed easily. "You think I have a chance to be elected to the That Sings Chosen Ones Hall of Fame?"

Kee Nang giggled. "Yes. I certainly think so."

"I couldn't have succeeded without your help," Chandler said seriously.

"Without you, the world would have been lost."

"Also, I couldn't have succeeded without the help of your father." Chandler reached up and absently touched the medallion that still hung around his neck; the tin and string had turned to gold. "He told me there were three things I had to do. I was so terrified at the end that I forgot all about them—but it seems I did them anyway."

"Yes," Kee Nang replied simply.

"I trusted someone I had no reason to trust."

Kee Nang nodded. "Til, the giant."

"I made a promise to someone I'd just met."

The woman reached around Chandler's back and rubbed the little boy's back. "You promised the *Gompen Tarma* that he would be all right."

Now Chandler turned to face Kee Nang and stroked her cheek with the back of his hand. Then he gently kissed her on the lips. "And the third command: I love you, Kee Nang."

"And I love you," Kee Nang replied, kissing him

back. "For you to love someone who loved you in return was always the easiest command to obey."

"I hadn't dared hope . . . Do you think we'll ever . . . ?" Chandler did not want to finish the question, did not want it to be finished. He dropped his gaze.

"If you're asking me if I'll come back, the answer is yes. In fact, I bought a round-trip ticket. Right after I take the *Gompen Tarma* home and visit with my parents, I'll return to you. If you want me."

Chandler grinned, reached into his pocket—and took out a piece of the bright, yellow fruit of the Loquat tree. He bit into it and grimaced—but he chewed and swallowed.

"Ah," Chandler sighed, grinning at Kee Nang and the boy, who grinned back at him. "Life is sweet."